Dark Moon
Lilith

Witches Anonymous, Step 4

Misty Evans

This book is dedicated to all the Team Luc fans.

ACKNOWLEDGMENTS

Many thanks to all who entered
the Name the Witch contest for Dark Moon Lilith:

Marilyn Wigglesworth – winner! (Mikayla)
Alexis Chapman – honorable mention (Nikita)
Christiana Tegethoff – honorable mention (Kitanna)
Natasha Jennex – honorable mention (Natasha)
Colette Chmiel, Christine Stack, Kaitlyn Stack, Emory Stankovits, Ashley
Stankovits, Susan Summers, Lise' Brandt, Barrie, Christine Nottling, Lisa
Pollard, Raonaid Luckwell, Robin Keenan, Krissy Philips, Ruth Thompson,
Abby Limback, Linda, Jackie Wisherd, Elizabeth Cerna, Jacki Chase, Dawn
Schugel, Wanda, Bridget Wolfe, Dena W., Pam K., Linda Bass, Queen Etain,
Michelle, Patricia Cochran, Lexee Toste.

I appreciate all of you entering the contest and helping me spread the word
about my stories. You're all winners in my book. If I've left anyone out,
please let me know and I'll add you!

Many thanks go to Judith Kerry and Michelle Miles for their awesome
support, excellent Twitter posts, and for editing this story for me. My days are
much more fun because of the two of you!

CHAPTER ONE

Love sucks. Just when you think you've got control of your heart, *wham*! A crystal vase filled with ruby red roses and purple dahlias—your favorite flowers—shows up on your doorstep.

Or in this case, at your ice cream shop.

Tucked inside the center of each gorgeous flower is a perfect Dove dark chocolate square.

Which reminds you that your boyfriend, who recently stomped on your heart, is really a very considerate fellow. He knows your likes and dislikes. He knows your weaknesses, but doesn't judge them. He wants to make amends for not showing up to your Witches Anonymous six-month magic-free anniversary celebration.

So your heart melts a little.

But then there's the other guy. Your ex.

He's seated in a corner booth wearing a black t-shirt and worn jeans, talking to his brother while he ignores you. He laughs and your skin tingles. He thumps the table with a fist and you jump. He slides over to lean his back against the wall and puts his feet on the booth seat, and instead of yelling at him to get his black boots off the red vinyl, you think how damn sexy he looks in all that black and break into a sweat.

I mean, really, who wears black when it's ninety degrees outside?

Someone who's used to the heat, that's who. Heat is one of the things my ex revels in.

Oh, and his gift of the day? A dirty banana-split bowl left on the edge of the table waiting for me to clean up.

Like I said—love sucks.

Noise from a kid's birthday party jangled my already taut nerves as I stared at Luc's dirty bowl. A dozen six-year-olds ran helter-skelter through the shop with only the birthday boy's parents trying to corral them. Mr. and Mrs. Duncan had pretty much given up thirty seconds into the party, though, so crowd control was officially AWOL. I'd given up in five, so I had to hand it to them for hanging in there that long.

Birthday parties were the latest installment in my brand new business plan to bring more customers to Evie's Ice Cream Shop. The economy sucked as bad as my love life and the first thing to go from most people's budgets seemed to be ice cream. Kids, however, didn't stop having birthdays when the economy went south, and parents would drain a vein in order to make Suzie or Bobby's day special. Hence, my genius idea to rent out the shop for parties, complete with ice cream cake and a magician to perform tricks.

Having been in Witches Anonymous for nearly eight months, I wasn't the one doling out the magic, however. I'd blackmailed Keisha, my best friend and the shop's manager, into that duty.

Evil of me, you say? Yep, that's me. Evil ex-witch trying to stick to her magic-free oath and make a living at the same time.

"Dark moon sure has everybody stirred up," Keisha said, eyeing the chaotic kids. Kinky tendrils of hair formed a copper-streaked halo around her head. A complimentary bright orange dress hugged her bodacious curves, over which she'd added a pretty white linen apron.

Behind the counter, I cringed as the children's shouts reached a crescendo. Even then, with all that high-pitched noise, Luc's low, seductive laughter wove its way through the din as if my ears were especially tuned to its erotic sound. I ignored the gooseflesh rising on my skin and gave Keisha a hip bump. "Magic time. Go get 'em, tiger."

She arched a brow and placed a hand on her orange-clad hip. The other hand squeezed a cotton dishtowel she'd been using to wipe down tables. Squeezing it so hard, her knuckles turned white. Reflected in her eyes was my neck under her fingers. "Amy Atwood, you may be my boss, but I'm not a common magician."

I gave her my most sincere, *take one for the team* smile. "Of course not. You're an extraordinary voodoo priestess, who could turn all those little kids into toads. But instead of using your powers for evil, you're using them for good today, and saving your best friend's sanity while also saving your own job."

Her lips crooked to one side as she considered the underlying warning. No magic show and we could kiss half the party fee goodbye. That fee was going to pay the electric bill, which for an ice cream shop in June is substantial. No electricity equaled the unemployment line for both of us.

"I do this and I get a bonus."

"Cash?" I shook my head. "I'm allowing your boyfriend to live in the back of the shop and sponge off me. That's part of the reason Evie's is going under. He eats ice cream like Adam's extended-cab truck guzzles gas, and since revenue is so low right now, that's the only bonus I can offer."

Her gaze slid to Gabriel who was still entertaining Luc in the corner booth. Gabe waved his hands in the air and yelled something in Latin, and Lucifer—yes, *that* Lucifer, Gabe's fallen-angel brother and my ex-boyfriend— wiped tears from the corners of his eyes, his body shaking with mirth.

They looked so happy, both of them, reunited again after Gabe took a walk on the wild side and ended up here on Earth with the rest of us.

Practically inseparable for the past two months, he'd spent his time bringing Luc up to speed on the goings on in Heaven and Luc helped Gabe blend in with us Earthlings. Hiding angel wings is no small feat, much less trying to merge a seven-foot tall, curly blond-haired guy with an attitude to match the width of his wings, into the normal citizenship of the town of Eden.

Keisha's shoulders, stiff with indignation, softened. The irritation left her face. Gabe had never had a girlfriend, and Keisha was way outside the lines of normal, so they'd logged some quality supernatural weirdness time with each other.

But who was I to talk? My ex was the Devil and my current boyfriend was the original Adam sent back to Earth for a redo. So while I was determined to stay magic-free and act like a human instead of a wicked, bad-to-the-bone witch, I was having a hard time coloring inside the lines of normal myself.

The one thing I *was* good at was using Gabe as a tool to manipulate Keisha into performing magic tricks at birthday parties.

What? I told you I was bad. And I couldn't stand the thought of losing my shop. It had been in my family for generations. I'd never known my father's side of the family, and this ice cream shop and my sister Emilia were all I had left of my mother's side. Well, my mother was still out there somewhere. I just didn't know where. She'd left me and Em with our aunt before I turned five years old and neither of us had seen her since. A part of me believed she was dead. Another part hoped she was alive and safe, even if she had provided us with prescription-grade abandonment issues.

"Fine." Keisha threw down the dishtowel and stomped around the end of the display freezer. She held up her hands in front of the rugrats, called for attention, and got nowhere. The kids didn't even glance her way.

She hooked a glare at me over her shoulder, her skeleton earrings swinging wildly. *What do I do now?*

I gave her an encouraging nod and made meaningless hand motions in an effort to get her to try again. She gave me a flippant eye roll and shook her head. *Screw this.*

Sighing, I inserted my pinkie and index fingers into the corners of my mouth and pierced the birthday party noise with a sharp whistle. Everyone, including Gabe and Lucifer, whipped their heads around to look at me.

Ahhh, utter silence. Much better.

Birthday boy had frozen with a spoonful of ice cream cake halfway to his mouth. "Whoa. Cool!" He'd destroyed several napkin holders and broken the leg off one of the chairs. A mental tab ran in the back of my mind to add to the party fee.

Leaving the security of the freezer, I sidled up next to Keisha and floated my hands around her, doing my best Vanna White impression. "And now munchkins, focus your eyes on the spectacular...on the amazing...on the magical...Voudini!"

A deep line appeared on Keisha's forehead. In the back of my mind, I heard her say, *Voudini? Seriously? That's the best you got?*

Cut me some slack, already. I was working on the spur of the moment and Voudini had a magic-y ring to it. Besides the fact, she was a voodoo priestess. It all worked together in my mind.

I clapped my hands at her. "Chop, chop, Amazing Voudini. Wow us with your spectacular magic show."

She narrowed her dark eyes at me and I swear I saw impending death reflected in them. There'd be hell to pay later, but I'd gladly pay if it meant shutting up the children for five minutes. Not that I don't like kids. I don't have any, so I can't be sure, but I *think* I like them. Just not a herd of them hopped up on sugar in my ice cream shop breaking things. My new business plan obviously needed tweaking.

Luc and Gabe were still staring at me, so I used the moment to my advantage. I strolled over to the vase of flowers, sniffed a rose with relish and took my time unwrapping one of the Dove chocolates before slipping it into my mouth. A round of oohs and aahhs rose from the kids as Keisha snapped her fingers and produced a baby chicken in the palm of one hand.

Voodoo witches and their chickens. Yeesh.

I smiled at Luc, picked up the vase, and made a show of carrying the flowers back to my office, swaying my hips just enough to feel his power rising around me as I walked away.

Passing Keisha, I gave her a sharp reminder. "No animals, Amazing Voudini. Health department rules."

The chicken disappeared to a second round of oohs and ahhs. Satisfied I wouldn't be undergoing another run-in with the health inspector any time soon, and with the fact I could still snag Luc's attention, I continued the hip-swaying foray toward my office. Once there, I opened the door and stopped dead in my tracks, nearly dropping the vase.

Waiting for me on the other side of my desk was an angel I thought I'd never see again.

Hoped I'd never see again.

Cephiel rose from the desk chair and held out his hands as if to embrace me. "Amy, my dear. How are you?"

CHAPTER TWO

Like usual, Cephiel was posing as Father Leonard, dressed in priest attire from head to toe, and giving me that serene priestly face he'd perfected.

For half a second, my brain backfired, and my heart, happy to see him, skipped with joy.

I'd missed him. He'd been my Witches Anonymous sponsor for several months, and the closest thing I'd ever had to a father—a real father, not a symbolic one—and the little girl inside me wanted to walk into his outstretched arms for an embrace.

He was no priest, though, and no father either. What he was, was a consummate actor and my guardian angel. Not the romantic kind of guardian angel books and movies portray. No, this one had lied, tricked, and manipulated me, along with Gabriel and Lucifer, all in the name of God.

"Get out."

His priestly smile turned patient. "How is step four going for you?"

Step four of Witches Anonymous involved examining my moral character in depth. Virtues, habits and behaviors. The good, the bad and the ugly. If you looked at my life over the past twenty-seven years, the bad far outweighed the good. I was trying to make up for that now, but it wasn't easy.

Especially when Luc wore black.

In truth, I preferred not to examine my moral character too much. Focus on the positive, right? Isn't that what all the self-help experts recommended? What good did it do to spotlight the fact I lacked integrity, honesty and morality? That I had a lot of bad habits?

And my behavior? Well, I'd been the Devil's right hand witch for seven years. Bad was my middle name, as much a part of my blood as my magic.

During the time Cephiel had been my WA sponsor and confidant, I'd believed I might actually have a few good qualities. That I could change my bad habits and improve my overall behavior. I had the moral fiber, as they say, I just needed regular reminders I could be good instead of evil.

However, one of my very worst qualities is being stubborn to the point of stupidity.

"Is this where I say I need your help with step four?" I snorted. "Forget that. I don't need anybody's help, thank you very much."

Cephiel skirted my desk and turned his hands up in supplication. "Please, Amy. Hear me out. Something bad is about to happen, and you are going to need my help."

Something bad was about to happen all right. He was lucky I was a still member of Witches Anonymous and had sworn an oath not to use magic, good, bad or otherwise. Even though I was on probation for another four weeks, thanks to him, I remained true to the oath and my commitment.

He was also lucky my hands were full with the vase of flowers. The idea of breaking it over his head crossed my mind, but that would be a waste of beautiful flowers and good chocolate.

"Maybe you didn't hear me the first time. Get out."

"You have every right to be angry, but I've come to make amends."

"Okay." I set the vase down and took a Keisha stance, hands on hips. "You can start by allowing Gabriel to return to Heaven."

Cephiel smiled that Father Leonard smile that said I was still young and ignorant while he was mature and wise. It reminded me of all the times he'd seemed to be my friend, guiding me through steps two and three of Witches Anonymous and my craptastic dealings with angels, demons and spells gone wonky.

He *was* mature and wise compared to me, but now that I knew he was a manipulative angel instead of my friend, I found it annoying rather than reassuring. "Gabriel is free to return to Heaven whenever he chooses."

Right. Nice try. "So why hasn't he?"

"Perhaps he doesn't want to."

The thought gave me pause. Angelzilla—my pet name for Gabe—did seem pretty happy here. He had a place to stay, unlimited trips to the ice cream buffet, Keisha to learn tantric sex from—bet they don't teach that in Heaven—and Lucifer to laugh at his jokes.

Sin, in other words, had a hold on him. Lust, gluttony, pride...he was enjoying them all.

If Cephiel was telling the truth, Gabe had the choice now whether to stay or go. I'm big on free will, after having my soul split in half for awhile and owned by Gabe and Luc in equal parts, so that was important. "Good. You can go then. I have no further need for your meddling."

Cephiel shook his head. "They warned me you'd be difficult about this, but your life and your soul are in danger. I'm afraid I'm not going anywhere. My job is to take care of you."

There were so many issues with that statement, I wasn't sure where to begin. I snapped another Dove from a rose, ripped off the wrapping and stuck the whole thing in my mouth.

Which was a stupid thing to do when I had a lot I wanted to say, so I half-chewed, half-swallowed and started talking with my mouth still full because indignation didn't give a flying fig about manners. "They? Who are *they*? And me, difficult? You haven't seen difficult yet, buster, and just for your information, my life hasn't exactly been a dish of vanilla ice cream. I've been taking care of myself, and doing a damn good job of it, since I started walking. From what I've seen, you haven't guarded me from anything, Mr. Guardian Angel." I made air quotes around the last words. "All you've done, in fact, is cause me more problems."

"A guardian angel isn't a bodyguard. My job is to help you make better decisions. Good choices instead of bad."

"I don't need help making better choices. I need help paying the bills. Getting off probation. Cleaning up my beautiful ice cream shop after Destructo Boy and his friends out there are gone. You gonna help with that?"

Father Leonard—Cephiel, I corrected myself (would I ever stop thinking of him as my sponsor and friend?)—opened his mouth to say something, but the door to the office blew open, and Keisha, eyes wide with urgency, interrupted. "Amy, I need you out here. Now."

Oh, great. What had the spawns of Satan done now? I glanced at my watch. We still had to entertain them for another forty minutes.

I'd had some circumstances in the past eight months that had tried my patience and determination to stay magic-free to the umpteenth degree. Would a dozen six-year-olds finally be the straw that broke me?

Somewhat grateful for any interruption that would get me away from Cephiel, I motioned for him to follow Keisha out. "There are plenty of people in the world who need your help." If the birthday boy had ruined another chair or napkin dispenser, he was going to be one of them. "I, however, don't."

Napkins littered the black and white tiles of the shop floor, the framed posters of various ice cream treats hung askew. Kids were still screaming, the adult Duncans huddled in the back pretending not to notice, and fudge sauce dripped off the potted fichus tree in the corner.

Let me tell you, paying the electric bill seemed highly overrated.

Keisha caught my eyes and jerked her head toward the cash register. A young woman stood at the counter wearing a pink sundress and blonde pigtails. Soft green eyes, open and friendly, peeked over her shoulder at me and a light sprinkling of freckles dotted her nose and cheeks. She couldn't have been more than sixteen or seventeen. Around her neck hung a trio of charms on a long chain and a stack of friendship bracelets climbed her left arm.

Glancing around, I checked to see if there was a Hansel to her Gretel. In the past, I'd had biblical characters show up in my shop. Fairy tale characters weren't too farfetched.

There was no Hansel in sight, so I breathed a sigh of relief and started forward again.

Potent energy hit me the moment I stepped in her direction. The magic imprisoned inside my chest did a weird back and forth *cha-cha*, wanting to reach out to her at the same time it wanted to push her away. She was hot as burning coals and icy as the frost inside the shop's freezer. A fresh spring meadow and an ancient, decrepit cemetery.

I pulled up short, cold sweat breaking out along my hairline. My stomach cramped at the same time a tendril of my magic escaped its prison and lunged for her.

The girl in front of me was a nascent witch.

She was either about to come into her powers or had just come into them and was confused about her abilities. Neither good nor bad yet, she was powerful all the same with unused magic just begging me to suck it up.

Pretending I couldn't feel the lure of her enchanting magic, I walked up to the cash register and forced my best Father Leonard-like smile. At the same time, I smothered my magic and stuffed it back inside its prison. "May I help you?"

She held out the *Eden Times* classifieds section and pointed to an ad circled in red pen under Employment Opportunities. "I'm here about the job."

The job. Of course.

What job?

CHAPTER THREE

Confused, I glanced at the black type ringed in red. I hadn't placed any help wanted ads, so there had to be some mistake. Maybe a different ice cream shop was looking for help. But that couldn't be either. Evie's was the only ice cream parlor in Eden.

Keisha sidled up beside Gretel and crossed her arms over her chest. "You won't give The Amazing Voudini a bonus, but you'll hire extra counter help?"

The girl's magic seeped into my skin, warming it at the same time it raised gooseflesh on my arms. I breathed deep, the smell of innocent magic making the other smells of the shop fuzzy. Couldn't Keisha feel the nascent witch's magic? She seemed oblivious.

"I didn't place any ad." I shrugged my shoulders at the girl, going for nonchalant even as I gripped the edge of the counter to keep my hands from reaching for her. "There must be some mix-up. We're not looking to hire anyone at this time."

The birthday boy ran up to Gretel and tugged at her sundress, his chocolate-stained hand leaving disgusting fingerprints on the pink cotton. "Hey, do you know how to do the Chicken Dance?"

She glanced down and smiled at him like he was a cute golden retriever puppy instead of the child from Hell. "The Chicken Dance is for babies and old people. I know the Space Ninja Dance. Want me to show you?"

"Space ninjas! Awesome!" He jumped up and down, and a second later, Gretel had two neat rows of quiet children lined up and mimicking her every move as she taught them ninja positions in slow-motion. The birthday boy's parents, along with Keisha, turned delighted gazes on me.

"You might want to reconsider that job opening," Keisha said under her breath as peace and tranquility returned to the shop.

I picked up the newspaper and studied the ad. Surprisingly, the shop's name and address were clearly listed. Hmmm. Who would place a help wanted ad in the *Eden Times* for my shop and why? Was it coincidence that a nascent witch would be the person to answer the ad?

I'm actually one of the few people in the world who believes in coincidence. The universe is too random in my opinion not to have them. In this case, however, my scalp tingled and my stomach was still uncomfortably tight, both warning me I was dealing with heavenly intervention.

9

Cephiel, surprise, surprise, had conveniently disappeared. Was this part of the new game he was playing? My gaze landed on Lucifer and Gabriel, wondering if they'd noticed Gretel's magical status and were thinking the same thing I was.

They'd noticed, all right. Lucifer's dark eyes were fixed on the girl. He'd shifted to the end of the booth, one hand gripping the edge of the table as if he was ready to catapult across the room after her. The only thing holding him back appeared to be Angelzilla's massive hand, locked on Lucifer's bicep. Gabriel, too, was focused on the girl as she pretended to be a ninja in space. Their sheer absorption caused my already tight stomach to gyrate and the magic in my chest to bang against the bars I had imprisoned it with.

Lucifer wanted her. Wanted her pristine, untouched magic. Not only did the witch inside me register jealousy, the woman inside me did too.

A sickly heat spread through my veins, and my pulse beat thick and heavy in my ears. If the kids had still been making noise, the din would've been lost under my thundering heartbeat.

You can't have her, I mentally told Lucifer.

He'd always been able to read my mind, even after we'd broken up. Even after God, or some other entity high on the heavenly food chain, took the half of my soul Lucifer owned and returned it to me.

Lucifer's attention begrudgingly swung my way. He rose from the seat, breaking Gabriel's hold with little more than a swift tug. Chin lowered and eyes glowering, he took his time walking to the counter, his movements like those of a large, wild cat stalking its prey. It was everything I could do not to take a step back as he reached the counter and confronted me.

Setting his fists on the laminated countertop, he leaned in and spoke sotto voce. "An eye for an eye, a soul for a soul."

When they'd handed out the Devil's secret code phrases, someone left me out of the loop. For a second, I wished Father Leonard, even if he really was Cephiel, was there to translate. "Huh?"

"Stay out of this, Amy. Her soul is mine."

A wave of dizziness struck as his words sunk in. "You mean, because you lost my soul, you think you're entitled to hers?"

"Universal balance must be maintained."

"Bullshit," I whispered, so the kids wouldn't hear me swear. I glowered back at him, but the room began to spin and I had to lean over the counter to stay upright. The pounding in my ears intensified and my stomach cramped hard. "Ow!"

Luc was around the end of the counter in a flash, grabbing my upper arms and turning me to face him. "What's the matter? You're pale as death."

The heat of his hands burned my skin. My magic purred inside my chest, but my stomach flip-flopped, threatening to bring up the chocolates I'd just consumed.

"I think I need to sit down," I said.

Before the words were completely out of my mouth, I was falling.

CHAPTER FOUR

The next two hours, I spent on my knees in my apartment bathroom, bent over the toilet. Lucifer and Gabriel had managed to get me upstairs, and since Keisha couldn't leave the shop unattended, she'd called my sister Emilia to come take care of me.

"What did you have to eat today?" Em asked, wringing out a cold washcloth in the sink before handing it to me.

I sunk my face into the cool cloth and sat back against the tub, closing my eyes. "Just the usual. Cereal this morning, a chicken salad sandwich at lunch, a couple of Dove chocolates this afternoon."

"Must've been the sandwich. Probably spoiled meat."

The mention of meat caused another round of vomiting. There was nothing left in my stomach to throw up, so I dry heaved instead. My whole body ached and I felt close to passing out. "Not food poisoning. Nascent witch."

Em brushed a strand of hair away from my face and examined me as if I'd had a momentary lapse of sanity along with my sickness. "What are you talking about?"

I didn't want to answer. All I wanted to do was close my eyes and go to sleep for a long, long time. The image of the young woman doing ninja moves in slow motion pressed against the back of my eyelids like a weird dream.

Sliding down to lie on the floor, I laid my cheek on the cool tile. "Gretel. Lucifer wants her soul."

"O-*kay*." The tone in her voice was the same one she used when humoring me about my singing skills on karaoke night over at BJ's Bar and Grill. Seriously, I do a mean Joan Jett impression. Em's jealous because the best she can do is a watered down Celine Dion. "And what does that have to do with you getting sick?"

My head felt hollow. For a second or two, I couldn't find my brain. Opening my eyes, I tried to focus my thoughts as well as my eyesight. The flowers on Emilia's skirt suddenly turned into piranhas gnashing at my face. I slammed my eyes closed again. "I have to help her, Em."

She said something else, but I didn't hear it. Everything inside me shut down, waves of sleep washing over me. I gave in to it...

Waking later to the sound of Adam's voice hovering over me was like a wonderful dream. "Let's get you into bed."

In his second go-around on Earth, Adam is a firefighter. He's tall, well-muscled from his job and has that whole heroic air going on. His strong hands lifted me off the floor and he cradled me as he carried me to my bedroom. Emilia flitted around in the background, doing her normal sisterly clucking and making sure Adam had me under control. Then she disappeared with a smile on her face.

Chilled from my nap on the tile, I burrowed into his warm body and wished I could go back to sleep in his arms. "Thank you for the flowers."

He laid me on the bed, tucking the covers around me. They weren't a substitute for his solid, comforting presence. But then again, in my current state of clammy skin, matted hair and bad breath, I wasn't exactly prime cuddling material.

"What flowers?"

"The roses with the chocolates. They're beautiful."

Adam's normally soft brown eyes hardened. A muscle flexed in his jaw. "I didn't send flowers."

Momentarily confused, I scanned my memory, wondering if it was playing tricks on me. Gretel, Cephiel, the vase of flowers…the memories were all there, if a little fuzzy. There hadn't been a card, so I'd assumed Adam was the giver.

But if he hadn't sent the flowers, then who?

Lucifer.

Oops. Anything involving him was sure to put Adam on the defensive. Luc purposely hung out at the shop under the guise of catching up with Gabriel, but Adam was convinced his real mission was to get me back.

Adam was right.

Lucifer had been on that particular mission since the minute I broke up with him, and Adam and I had been on shaky ground since he'd missed my six month magic-free Witches Anonymous ceremony in April. Eve was back on Earth, too, and had managed to divert him from attending, and I'd been holding a grudge ever since. While Adam was convinced Luc was trying to win me back, I was convinced Eve was doing the same with him. We'd been circling each other and our past relationships for nearly two months and getting nowhere.

I'd thought the flowers were a peace offering.

They were, apparently.

Just not from Adam.

Flowers were rarely Luc's calling card, but he had been known to spring for them on occasion. The first time I met him, he'd laid a rose at the feet of the Venus di Milo statue in the Louvre in Paris, and the sight had sent my romantic heart into overdrive.

Adam frowned, seemingly angry and embarrassed that the flowers weren't from him. My limbs were too weak to move much, but I was able to touch his hand with mine. "Cephiel is playing games with me again. Probably one of his tricks."

A wary relief eased Adam's frown. I flinched as another cramp hit, and his eyes turned soft and concerned again. "Is there anything I can do for you?"

My cats, Cain and Abel, made an appearance, jumping on the bed and settling down in their normal spots. Seeing them reminded me of Luc and Gabriel.

Gretel, my mind chirped. I needed to protect her from Lucifer, but if her pure, innocent magic was going to affect me this strongly, I had to find someone else to help her. My choices were limited. Em had had her hands full, taking care of me and didn't understand what was at stake. Adam wasn't a witch or an angel. He was definitely hero material, but he was one-hundred-percent human. Not a supernatural bone in his body. Which was interesting since Eve had all kinds of witchy powers. "Get Keisha for me?"

He covered my hand with his and gave it a squeeze. "Are you sure you don't want to go a real doctor instead?"

I'd be better off in Keisha's hands than an MDs, especially since I hated doctors and hospitals. "I'm fine. I just need to talk to her."

Adam nodded. "I'll call you tomorrow."

Two minutes later, Emilia was running the shop and Keisha was at my bedside. "You look like I put a hex on you."

I sat up and rubbed my face with my hands. "I feel like it too."

"Emilia thinks your chicken salad was tainted, but you gave me half, and I'm not sick. You must have a stomach virus."

"It's Gretel. Didn't you feel her energy?"

"Of course I did. And her name is Mikayla. I was trying to play it cool in front of Luc." She gave me a sorry face. "Not that that worked."

Oh, no. "Please tell me he didn't already get her soul."

Keisha patted my leg and motioned me to scoot over. Once I made room for her, she perched on the edge of the bed. "I know I should have confirmed this with you first, but I hired her. Just a few hours a week so we can keep an eye on her for now. Her grandmother died a few months ago, and she's got no one else. She needs a job."

"She's too young to live alone."

"She's eighteen. Going to community college this fall. For now, she's downstairs filling out paperwork, and since you're out of commission, she's going to stick around and help me clean up the birthday party disaster."

The anxiety working under my skin lessened. "What about when she leaves the shop?"

Keisha bit a fingernail. "Guess I could follow her, try to keep her safe."

"Put Gabe on her. He's an archangel. He can protect her from Luc."

"He wants her magic too."

I dropped my head back onto the headboard. "Tell me you're kidding."

Keisha smoothed her skirt with shaky fingers, lips thinning. "Her pure magic can help him get back into Heaven."

The hurt in her voice was blatant. She had fallen for Gabe, hook line, and voodoo doll. I hoped Cephiel was right about what he'd told me earlier. "Your boy toy doesn't want to go back to heaven, K. He's had the power to return for months according to Cephiel. Gabe's sticking around for you."

Her big brown eyes lit with happiness. "Really?"

I nodded, glad I could relieve her worries. Problem was, that meant Gabe wanted Mikayla for some other reason.

A nascent witch was the golden egg to both good and evil. Powerful magic, untainted by either side, is the equivalent of pure gold, especially in someone like Mikayla who had made it past puberty without succumbing to it. The longer a natural born witch went without using her powers, the stronger they became.

The ways her magic could be used were endless. The ramifications, the consequences to her soul, also endless. And not healthy. In fact, the magical history books were filled with stories of entities using nascent witches to increase their powers and leaving the innocent witch to die, her soul forever bound to whatever entity had stripped her powers.

An idea flickered to life in the dim recesses of my mind. Dragging in a deep breath, I raked my fingers through my hair and motioned for Keisha to move off the bed.

"Where do you think you're going?" she said, giving me her superior African priestess glare.

"I have to talk to her."

The instant I put my feet on the floor, black dots danced in front of my vision. Keisha put both hands on my shoulders and gave a push. I flopped backwards into the sheets, too weak to resist. My head pounded and acid rose up my chest and into my throat. I curled into a ball and moaned.

Thank goodness Keisha already knew I was a wuss and loved me anyway so I didn't have to pretend otherwise. She shifted me around and talked me back under the covers. "You're not going anywhere. Get some sleep and I'll take care of Mikayla. By the way, her magic has nothing to do with you being sick. I'm telling you, you have a stomach virus."

"There's acid in my throat," I whined. "Can I have some water?"

She picked up an orange box of baking soda from the nightstand and fished out a tiny amount on the end of a spoon. Apparently Em had expected I'd need some natural medication. Em's Wiccan and all about natural. "Take this. It will help."

I'm not so big on *au naturale*. I made a face and shook my head.

"Amy, stop being bullheaded. You've thrown up so much, you've aggravated your stomach lining. The baking soda will neutralize the acid." She smiled, her coaxing smile, meant to reassure me. "You'll feel a lot better if you take this."

The white powder was thick on my tongue and I nearly gagged from the salty taste, but Keisha followed up with a glass of water, and after a few seconds, my mouth and throat felt cleaner. The burning sensation in my throat went away. I slumped down deep in the bed and she stroked my head like I was a little kid, brushing the hair out of my face and rubbing my temples in a circular, clockwise manner. The pounding in my head faded and I drifted off to sleep.

When I woke again, the room was dark except for the soft light of my bedside lamp. Cain and Abel snuggled around my body, sleeping peacefully. The warm smell of ginger and something else I couldn't name but hinted at jasmine, filled my nose. Breathing in deeply, I cracked my eyes open and found Cephiel sitting on a chair next to my bed, legs crossed and sipping from a cup of tea.

"I warned you," he said, uncrossing and recrossing his legs. "Summoned or not, the god will come."

Braggart. I had no idea what he was talking about—*the god will come*—but the smugness in his voice pissed me off. "While I hate throwing up, I hardly think a stomach virus requires guardian angel intervention."

He gave me an *I know something you don't* smile. "You know, if you weren't so busy being a smartass all the time, you might actually be more than a washed-up witch, running a failing ice cream parlor in a rinky-dink town in the Midwest."

Ah, so the gloves were coming off. This was a first. In all my dealings with Cephiel, he never once resorted to snarky put-downs.

But those were easier to handle than his ongoing disappointment in me and my behavior. I struggled to raise myself up on one elbow, easing Cain over. If I hadn't been so weak, I would have reached out and knocked Cephiel's tea straight into his face. "And if you weren't such a self-righteous prick, you might actually be a decent guardian angel. You'd at least have the balls and good conscience to protect a nascent witch, instead of sending her to me."

He sipped the tea as if he had all day to taunt me. "First of all, you don't have a stomach virus. You were poisoned by a Tox demon. An assassin, highly skilled. Secondly, I did you a favor, sending the nascent witch here. Lucifer can have her soul instead of yours, so all debts are paid." He snapped his fingers and another cup of tea appeared, this one on my nightstand. The heavenly smell teased my nose. "Drink, now. You're going to need your strength."

"For what?"

"To face Lilith."

My magic shuddered so hard inside my chest, my heart contracted. The rest of my body trembled in response.

And I had no idea why.

Pretty sure I didn't want to know, I asked anyway. "Who's Lilith?"

This time, Cephiel gave me a pleasant Father Leonard smile. "You know. *Lilith*. Queen of Hell. Mother of demons. Also widely known as, Lucifer's consort."

Oh, right. That Lilith.

Lucifer's consort.

Huh?

CHAPTER FIVE

Inside my chest, my magic swerved and swayed as if I'd given it a sleeping pill and it couldn't now rouse itself completely. My stomach was hollow and my eyes burned like I'd rubbed sand in them. I glanced at the tea, steaming innocently beside the bed. Something was out of place, but I couldn't quite put my finger on it. It wasn't anything to do with Lucifer or Lilith, though, that much I was sure of.

I struggled into a sitting position. "Tell me more about the Tox demon."

"Clever, that one." Cephiel stared into the mid-distance, not seeing my room anymore, but what he was seeing I couldn't be sure. Only that it pleased him. "Her name is Kitanna Ivey. If Lilith hired her, you know she's good. An expert. Knows you well enough to hit you with your greatest vice."

Good human or bad witch, last I checked, my greatest vice was lust. "I don't follow."

He glanced at me, raised a brow with impatience. "The chocolates in the roses. She poisoned the chocolates, knowing you can't refrain from eating them. Can't refrain from eating *all* of them. No self control. I mean, really, you have to hand it to her. Kitanna's exceptional at her job. If your friend hadn't interrupted, you'd be dead right now and in Hell, facing Lilith."

A new annoyance set up shop in my head. Nobody messed with my Doves, and Cephiel's admiration of a demon at my expense was damned irritating. "Why is Lilith trying to kill me?"

Again, an impatient, frustrated look crossed his face. If he'd been Keisha, he would have said, *get with the game, Amy*. Instead, he coaxed me up to speed. "Lucifer? Ring any bells?"

Boy, he was full of himself today, but a small, weak light bulb went on in the recesses of my brain. "You said Lilith is Luc's consort?" My voice quavered. "So, they had some kind of relationship?"

"Some kind of relationship?" He chuckled low, shook his head as if my brain were still two scoops short of a triple scoop cone. "You don't know your history very well, do you?"

My history was burned into my brain. No forgetting that. Lucifer's? I'd never cared much about it and he wasn't one to share. "Enlighten me."

Cephiel slid his attention to the cup on my nightstand. "Your tea is getting cold."

18

I ignored his pointed attempt to get me to drink. While I doubted there was angelic mojo in it, he'd tricked me before quite effectively and I didn't trust him. Once bitten, twice shy, and all that.

"Lucifer and I hooked up for seven years." We did a lot more than hook up, but accurate terminology seemed a moot point. "We also broke up eight months ago. Why is Lilith after me now?"

Leaning back in the chair, Cephiel took a long sip of his tea. Another light bulb in my brain sparked to life. Since when did he drink anything other than black coffee? I definitely wasn't touching that tea.

"Lucifer has engaged in a wide assortment of dalliances through the years, but he's always gone back to Lilith when he grew tired of them." He raised his cup in mock salute. "You, however, are more than a trifling affair."

Hearing about Luc's past love life made my skin itch. Damn right, I was more than a trifling affair, but that affair was over. Sort of. "I can't help he's still hanging around. It's not like I'm encouraging him. I have Adam now."

"Before Lilith was cast into Hell and became the mother of all demons, she was Adam's first…wife. Technically speaking."

A weary, humorless laugh escaped my parched lips. "I don't know what you're drinking there, Ceph, but *Eve* was Adam's wife, remember?"

"According to the King James Bible, yes, but there are pieces of history expunged from Genesis. Including the love triangle between Adam, Lilith and Lucifer. Even God Himself had a role in that sordid affair, but that part wouldn't play well with modern day Christians. Lilith disobeyed God long before Eve existed, was sent to Hell, and has ruled there ever since."

If Cephiel wanted to torture me, he was doing a damned good job. Thinking about either Adam or Lucifer with another woman made a sharp pain ricochet around my heart.

The angel was still playing games, though, and I'd never been a team player. Ask my kindergarten teacher. She'll tell you I was a lone wolf even back then. Rebellious and lousy at going along with anything others wanted to do.

I set my hands in my lap and mentally poked the magic inside my chest, trying to get it to wake up and help me figure out what Cephiel was up to. It refused to stir. I had to rely on my lousy human instincts. "Will the Tox demon come after me again, once she knows I'm still alive?"

A new steaming cup of tea appeared in my hands. I nearly bobbled it, grabbing the dainty handle just in time to keep it from spilling all over the blanket. Cain opened his eyes and hissed at Cephiel.

Cephiel made at face at Cain, uncrossed his legs and leaned forward in his chair. "Count on it."

The dormant magic in my chest jumped like I'd stuck a finger in a light socket and suddenly I knew it wasn't my guardian angel sitting next to my bed. Instincts, maybe, both magical and human, from my brain to my sixth sense, came online. He looked like Cephiel, but the entity in the chair didn't act or talk like him.

I threw the cup of tea at his face and the skin sizzled and burned where the liquid hit it, changing the features from Father Leonard's to something new. Some*one* new. As the facial features morphed into a different arrangement, the body followed suit.

Pale skin, celery green eyes and kinky red hair replaced Cephiel's short dark hair, olive-colored skin and hazel eyes. The black and white priest getup succumbed to neon green spandex, stretched tight over a woman's lithe body. Anchored in a belt along her waist were a row of short, skinny knives.

She stood, seeming unfazed by the transformation, and gave me an evil, malicious grin. I rolled toward the opposite side of the bed, over the cats, who were both hissing now, and came to my feet, swaying as a wave of dizziness hit along with instant recognition. "Kitanna Ivey?"

She drew a knife from the leather belt and ran the top of her nails along the edge, leaving a coating of green nail polish behind. "You're harder to kill than I expected."

She aimed the knife at my throat and I ducked, pushing on the top mattress and heaving as hard as I could—which wasn't that hard in my weakened state, but did send Cain and Abel scurrying through the air and screeching as they went. The knife made a sharp *ting* as it embedded itself in the wall but the sound was drowned out by Kitanna screaming like a banshee as the cats raced across her feet. She jumped up onto the chair, head down, gaze swinging wildly in all directions, looking for more feline evacuation.

That was my chance. I hopped up on the mattresses and launched myself at her. At the same time, I yelled, "Cephiel!"

I tackled her and we toppled over the chair, hitting the floor hard and knocking the breath out of both of us. Tangled in Kitanna's limbs, I was conscious of the belt of knives and fought to keep her hands away from them, but that meant her fingernails, with their wicked green acidic poison, brushed against my arms in multiple places. Everywhere the polish touched, it burned.

The pain faded into the background as we fought. She was my size but wiry, and since I wasn't well versed in all-star wrestling moves, she easily rolled me off and pinned me against the wall in a few seconds flat.

"I hate cats," she said, panting, and grabbing a chunk of my hair.

She gave a hard yank and tears stung my eyes. My limbs shook with a combination of adrenaline and exhaustion. Waves of pain burned my arm, one spot especially hot from a concentration of her polish. "Don't take this personally, but I could care less."

A bright light burst into the room and I took advantage of the distraction to knee her in the groin. Yeah, I know, she was female, but I thought she had balls, even if they were only metaphorical ones, to come into my house and try to poison me while posing as Father Leonard.

She grunted and freed a knife from her belt, but before she could sink the poisonous blade into my chest, Cephiel appeared. He snagged the box of open baking soda from my nightstand and tossed it to me.

Baking soda. Cuts acid, Keisha had said. Would it work on poisonous nail polish?

I started to shake it at Kitanna, and she slapped it away, the box flying out of my grip. But a wave of Cephiel's hand made it fly right back. Point to the guardian angel.

Kitanna kicked me in the stomach and the action jarred the box. Baking soda exploded from the open end and fell in a white cloud of powder all over her.

Her eyes went wide and a heartbeat later, she began to sizzle and melt.

Her hand released my hair, skin liquefying and muscles, tendons and bones beginning an ugly disintegration. She cried out in pain, twisting this way and that as I backed up tight against the wall, watching her disappear inch by green gooey inch in a macabre version of the Wicked Witch's death throes.

"When you get back to where you came from," I said, holding my wounded arm, "tell Lilith I said hi."

Her eyes narrowed with menace just before they softened and joined the rest of her, finally, completely liquefying into a mass of sticky-looking green goo.

Even her knife blades and leather belt went from solid forms into runny juice. The only thing marking where she'd been was filmy green fluid puddled on my floor. Cephiel reached over and offered me a hand. I didn't want to take it, but I relented, my magic pressing me to get away from Kitanna's remains.

"Don't touch that," Cephiel said. "It's poisonous."

"No shit, Sherlock."

He looked me over with a critical eye. "*Thank you* would be a more appropriate response after I just saved your life."

I showed him my appreciation with one of my fingers.

CHAPTER SIX

Two a.m., I stood inside the main entrance to Eden's fire station, trying to convince the lone firefighter manning the desk —his name tag read *Rowen,* and his crew cut and freckles made me think he'd be the perfect Hansel to Mikayla's Gretel—to wake Adam. He told me he wasn't even sure Adam was on duty, but my Spidey sense said Adam was asleep upstairs and the young rookie fire fighter who'd drawn the short straw for desk duty didn't want to wake him up.

"This is an emergency," I told the kid and held up my bandaged arm for emphasis even though that wasn't the reason I was there. Any time you start waving injured limbs in front of trained emergency personnel, they get jumpy. "I need to talk to him. Now."

Whether it was the tone of my voice, the bandaged arm or the fact I looked like a zombie, Rowen relented, trudging up the stairs and returning with a half-asleep Adam in tow a few minutes later.

Clear concern etched Adam's face, hair a spiked disaster on top of his head. Without hesitation, he drew me in close, wrapped his arms around me. "Ames? What happened to your arm? Are you okay?"

A false sense of peace washed over me. I rested my ear against his chest to listen to his heartbeat. Solid, steady, it further lulled me into a serene contentment I wished I could hang on to.

When I didn't answer, though, Adam set me back a few inches, looking me over from head to toe. Cephiel had fed me applesauce and toast, confirmed there had been a lot of history between God, Lilith, Adam and Lucifer, and argued with me about taking care of Mikayla. In the end, though, my head had cleared enough to blackmail him into pulling his bodyguard routine on her in exchange for me allowing him to coach me in my new quest to take on Lilith.

He thought he'd help me make some of those wise choices he was so keen on.

Right.

Regardless of Cephiel's warnings and what I'd just been through with Kitanna, my magic was fully awake and beating its clawed fists against the prison bars in my chest. It wanted to take on the Queen of Hell with no preparation for what I might be facing and a total disregard of her immense supernatural powers.

In other words, it was pissed.

My heart, however, was a bit on the prickly side, and wanted answers about the love triangle Kitanna had mentioned. I'd almost called Luc and asked him about it, but the voice inside my head told me I couldn't handle seeing him right then. Adam was a safer bet all the way around.

Now that I was here, though, confronting Adam in the flesh, I hesitated. A part of me really didn't want to know the biblical soap-opera details. That past was literally ancient history and shouldn't have mattered one little bit. Unfortunately, I was now in Lilith's line of fire, and the only way I could figure out how to get off the center of her target was to understand exactly what had gone on In The Beginning.

"Tell me about..." My voice cracked. Inside my diaphragm, an invisible hand shoved the words up my esophagus, but my mouth didn't want to form Lilith's name. I cleared my throat and drew Adam farther away from Rowen's hearing. "About you and Eve and...Lilith."

I expected the lift of an eyebrow, a widening of his eyes, an open mouthed gape—some tell-tale sign suggesting he was surprised I knew about the three of them. What I saw instead was a distinct hardening of his features.

His jaw firmed, his lips tightened. "He couldn't resist, could he? He had to bring up Lilith and make me look bad." Jamming his fingers through his hair, he paced away from me. "Next time I see him, I swear I'm going to kill that SOB."

Confused, I could only stare. "Who? Cephiel?"

Adam crossed back to me in two steps, eyes blazing with hate. "Lucifer."

"Lucifer isn't the one who told me about you and Lilith."

Surprise finally made an appearance. "He didn't?"

Just as I started to tell him about the Tox demon, a loud clanging echoed through the station, bouncing off the walls and vibrating inside my head with way too much intensity after my recent illness. Er, poisoning.

The fire alarm.

Talk about Pavlov's dogs and stimuli, the fire station's occupants went into emergency response mode like well-trained experiments. Adam gave me his sorry face and began to back away as the fire station came to life all around us. Lights flickered on, Rowen snatched up a microphone on the desk's two-way radio and relayed information about the fire and its location over the loudspeaker. As Adam disappeared up the stairs to grab his clothes, half-dressed and sleepy-eyed men came sliding down the fire pole, running to various trucks the moment their feet touched the concrete floor.

The blare of the fire alarm continued to echo in my head and my strength left me. I sagged onto a lonely chair near Rowen's desk and plugged my ears with my fingers. The giant garage doors creaked and rattled as they rose to allow the waiting trucks to escape. Before the interior alarm stopped, the fire engine sirens started. I hunched over, setting my elbows on my knees, and closing my eyes, fingers still in my ears against the onslaught.

Next thing I knew, Adam was shaking me. I looked up to find him bent over me in full gear. "What are you doing?" he yelled over the sirens.

Seemed pretty obvious. I'd been poisoned, attacked and had found out my boyfriend had once been the Queen of Hell's husband. Besides that fact, my *ex*-boyfriend had apparently also spent some quality time with her. Maybe still was. Maybe during the seven years Lucifer and I had been together, he'd been going home to her every night.

I raised my hands, palms up, and glared at Adam. *Haven't you ever seen a tired, pissed off ex-witch before?*

He lifted me out of the chair. "The fire, Amy. Didn't you hear the address?"

A spark of comprehension flashed inside me. I hadn't heard the address over the blare of the alarm, but the look on his face confirmed my hunch. My stomach dropped and I numbly shook my head, more in denial than in answer.

"It's your apartment. Your building is on fire."

My apartment.

A dozen questions flew through my mind, but all I could see were the faces of my cats. "Cain and Abel!"

Adam hauled me toward the last fire truck where it waited for him, and yanked open the cab door. He shoved me up into the high seat, my heart going a mile a minute in fear.

Before he could even close the door, the driver nailed the accelerator and we shot out of the station house and into the dark night.

CHAPTER SEVEN

Fire had always enchanted me. The orange-yellow flames, the wispy smoke, the smell of burning wood… my air magic called to it, seductive and tantalizing.

Watching it eat my upstairs apartment, however, sickened me. The flames shooting out the broken windows weren't normal. Instead of orange, red and yellow, they were black and shiny as silk, a putrid fluorescent blue edge to them. They flowed up the sides of the second floor and onto the roof, burning away the metal, wood and shingles on the outside as effectively as I was sure they were burning up the inside. The water the firemen poured onto the fire was useless. The flames continued to spread, hot and out of control. Within a few short minutes, my apartment folded in on itself, the roof collapsing and the carefully placed support beams twisting and falling in a macabre slow motion dance.

Adam and another fire fighter attempted to rescue the cats. The fire, however, leapt and hissed down at them when they tried to enter the ice cream shop's front entrance, driving them back. Adam shouted at me not to give up hope before he disappeared into the alley behind the shop to try the metal fire escape at the back of the building.

I sent mental and quiet verbal pleas to Cephiel for help. He didn't show.

Keisha, who lived three short blocks north, had heard the sirens and arrived shortly after us. She stood beside me now, one arm around my shoulders for support as tears rolled down my face at the thought of my poor kitties being stuck and defenseless against the evil fire. Gabriel, who'd been with her at her condo, stood on my other side, not saying a word but exuding his normal reserved uppity-ness.

I wanted to strike out at him. To demand why he hadn't been in his room in the back of the ice cream shop so he could have stopped the fire. At the very least, he could have saved my cats.

But, bottom line, none of this could be laid at Angelzilla's feet, no matter how annoying he was.

"This is all my fault," I said, unable to take my eyes off the blue-black flames. "Cephiel warned me something bad was going to happen. I should have taken him more seriously. If nothing else, I should have protected Cain and Abel."

25

Keisha squeezed my uninjured arm. "This is dark moon magic. You're just lucky you weren't home or you'd be dead."

A dark moon signified the darkest night of the month, a time when even certain good witches set their dark sides free. Some practiced contrary magic, reversing the normal order of things and participating in binding and cursing rituals. Others contacted the dead, or changed themselves into dark animals in order to roam the night without detection and interact with baneful spirits.

Baneful spirits like Tox demons and Pyro demons.

A seed of fury unfurled inside me. I glanced to the left and then to the right, up and down the sidewalks, scanning the openings to various alleys and the shadowed spaces between buildings. The aftermath of the poisoning had left me lightheaded and my vision a touch blurry if I moved my head too fast, but I could've sworn I saw unnatural shadows everywhere I looked. "Lilith."

Keisha's voice echoed mine with a hint of skepticism. "Lilith?"

I brushed the tears off my cheeks. Queen of Hell or not, the bitch was going down. "She had a Tox demon poison my Dove chocolates, the ones in the flowers that were delivered today? When that didn't do the job, the Tox demon came back and attacked me." I showed her my bandaged arm. "Now, if my guess is right, Lilith sent a Pyro demon to roast me."

A group had gathered on the sidewalk around us, watching my apartment burn and gossiping behind their hands. Some were other store owners in the neighborhood, making sure their businesses were safe, and a few were customers, wondering if the ice cream shop was going to burn too. Among those were the sensation seekers, simply there to gawk.

The flames destroying my apartment had not migrated downstairs to the ice cream parlor. Except for the fire dipping down to fend off Adam from entering the shop, the flames appeared content to only burn the upstairs, but the water and smoke were probably destroying the ice cream shop anyway.

Glancing over her shoulder, Keisha drew me away from the throng to a nearby bench under an old oak tree. Gabe reluctantly followed as she guided me into the seat. "Tox demon? Lilith? I thought you had a stomach virus."

"You were wrong, Doc. I was poisoned. The Tox demon told me Lilith hired her." I scanned the crowd, looking for anyone who stood out from the normal citizens of Eden. The Pyro had failed to kill me, which meant he or she would try again. Or some other demon on Lilith's payroll would. "Apparently the Queen of Hell has decided she wants Lucifer back and the easiest way to make that happen is to get rid of me. Permanently."

Over the heads of the crowd, I caught sight of movement on the far sidewalk. Movement that was too graceful, too otherworldly to be human. Dressed in black, but not one of the unnatural shadows that darted and scurried in my peripheral vision.

The magic in my chest mewed loudly and I shot up off the bench. Lucifer's gaze met mine as he strode under a street lamp, blue-black hair reflecting the light.

Running alongside his booted feet, were two furballs with matching long hair and smooshed-in faces.

"Cain! Abel!" I took off at a sprint, the cats' frantic meows reaching my ears over the sounds of the crowd, crackling fire, and pumping water. I dropped to my knees as the cats reached me halfway and gathered them into my arms, burying my nose in their Himalayan fur and talking absolute nonsense to both of them. The acrid smell of magical smoke hung on their coats and my hate for Lilith, a woman—demon? witch? evil bitch, for sure— I'd never met, ratcheted up a thousand times higher.

Luc gripped my upper arms and hauled me to my feet, the cats bailing as I looked up into his strained face. The black eyes underneath his dark eyebrows reflected light from the street lamp and emotions I rarely saw. Without saying a word, he crushed me to his body, wrapping his arms around me and burying his face in my hair, much like I'd done to Cain and Abel.

He didn't say a word, just held me, and my heart hammered like a hummingbird trapped inside my chest.

My magic purred in contentment, rising to meet the abject relief and happiness rolling off Luc's body and swirling around both of us. I swear, if my heart and magic had been in charge, I would have stayed in that exact spot forever.

Cain and Abel wove their chubby bodies around our ankles, and for a second, everything in my world seemed okay. "You rescued my cats."

One of Luc's hands slipped under my hair and cradled the back of my neck. He shifted his face to lean his forehead against mine. His breath was warm and soft against my skin. "Thank God, you're okay."

Hearing Luc reference God in such a manner sounded odd. Then again, it wasn't that Luc didn't believe in God. He was, after all, Luc's father. But I didn't think God had much to do with me being okay, even though He'd apparently tagged Cephiel as my guardian angel. The big guy had ulterior motives. He didn't care much about my health and well-being...he just wanted my soul.

Luc, on the other hand, cared about me enough to save my cats from being fricasseed. "How did you know my apartment was on fire?"

"Cain. He called me."

Cain had always favored Luc. Even now, he sat on the sidewalk next to Luc's right foot, rubbing his head against Luc's leg. "He *called* you?"

Luc was still holding me close, his thickly lashed gazed boring into mine as if he were afraid to blink for fear I'd disappear. "Telepathically. He was distressed."

Behind me, Keisha cleared her throat. I turned my head and found an audience watching us. Gaping was more like it. They'd all stopped talking and turned their attention from the fire to me and Luc.

Well, mostly Luc. He commands people's attention without even trying.

A skinny guy two rows back held up the cell phone and snapped a picture. Crap. Was Adam watching too?

Glancing toward the fire trucks, I scanned the men battling the magical fire. Underneath their helmets and turnout coats, I couldn't tell one from the other, but I didn't recognize Adam's broad shoulders or solid frame amongst those I could see.

Phew.

Although Adam wasn't watching us, everyone else was. I stepped back, gave Luc a nod, trying to appear properly friendly and nothing more. "Thank you for saving Cain and Abel."

He dropped his hands and the vulnerability on his face disappeared like it had never been there. "Sorry I couldn't extinguish the fire. It was…"

His gaze darted to the human contingent around us and back to me. *Magically enhanced*, he finished, using his own brand of mental communication. "I called 911."

A woman in the crowd, wearing a pale pink robe belted at the waist, stepped forward, eyes big and round and totally star-struck. "You're a hero!" She had a long, horse-like face, and her jowls jiggled as she nodded her head at those next to her and pointed at Luc. "An honest to God hero, right here in Eden!"

Others raised their voices in agreement and clapping started. The crowd surged forward, squeezing me and the cats out of the way to encircle Luc. Men patted him on the back. Women clasped their hands in front of their chests and ogled him. He craned his neck to keep me in sight, his face pleading for help.

I gathered up the cats and moseyed away from his new fan club, giving him a wink and a thumbs-up sign. Inside my head, he said, *don't you dare leave me with these…*

"Amy!" Emilia was running down the sidewalk, my friend Liddy and half a dozen other Witches Anonymous peers on her heels. In a town the size of Eden, word spreads fast.

Not so strangely absent from the group was my arch WA enemy, Marcia. Oddly enough with my apartment burning and my life in jeopardy, her annoying presence would still have been reassuring.

"What happened?" Emilia said. "Are you all right? Oh, my, goodness. How did the fire start? Were you asleep? How did you get out? What happened to your arm?"

Emilia continued her tirade without missing a step—or taking a breath— while the single last support beam inside my apartment fell to the ground and

28

disintegrated in a puff of black ash. Without preamble, the fire winked out. A gaping hole above the ice cream shop showed off the moonless night sky, cloudy with blue-tinged smoke.

Liddy put her arms around me and gave me a gentle hug, careful not to squash the cats or my arm. Abel twisted in my arms and reached for her, just like a toddler might have.

While Cain favored Luc, Abel knew Liddy was the winning lottery ticket of catdom. She brought him catnip toys, stroked his belly for hours at a time, and brought Hecate, her familiar, around to visit once or twice a week. Abel had it bad for the feline as well as her owner.

Lightning bolts of raw energy danced in between strands of her hair. Stress does that to her.

I patted her arm, trying to relieve some of that stress. "I'm okay, Liddy. Really."

Liar, liar, apartment on fire. I wasn't even close to okay. What I was close to was a total freak out, followed by a meltdown.

My hand trembled as I drew it away from Liddy's arm. I balled it into a fist and clenched my teeth. Freak-outs and meltdowns never achieved anything constructive, and they certainly weren't going to stop Lilith and her mercenaries.

Convinced the Pyro was still hanging around, I took another slow scan of the area. Shadows clinging to the alleys and buildings seemed less ominous, but unease slithered up my legs. A sharp achiness had set up shop in my back and ribs. My neck twinged with every movement. The violent vomiting I'd done earlier had left everything sore and throbbing. My mouth and throat, dry and raw.

The whole experience came crashing down on me. My life was being threatened, my place was gone. At that very moment, someone was planning my death. Someone who would do anything, even burn up a couple of innocent cats, to get to me. Every one of the people around me might be in danger.

I staggered to the bench.

Emilia, Liddy, Keisha and the others fluttered around me, asking me if I was okay, patting my back, asking me if I needed a glass of water, etc. Dots flickered in front of my eyes and I lay down on the bench, trying not to pass out. If the Pyro or Lilith were indeed watching, I'm sure the sight of me prone on the bench made them smile.

My magic screeched its anger and I swallowed hard against the indignation. *Laugh it up,* I told Lilith. *Your days are numbered.*

There was nothing I could do at that moment, though, to fight. My magic and my heart were willing, but my body wasn't.

The smell of strong coffee registered enough to make me open my eyes a few minutes later. Marilyn, the owner of a nearby restaurant, had been thoughtful enough to make coffee and was now handing out Styrofoam cups to anyone who wanted one. Keisha was waving one of the white cups under my nose.

"Yup," she said. "Works every time."

Somehow I managed to sit up and take the coffee. My stomach wasn't ready for anything, but the smell revived me enough, some of my brain cells began to fire.

Thinking, however, wasn't that much fun. There wasn't much to think about except the fire and the fact I was a sitting duck.

I caught Marilyn's eye in the crowd and smiled my thanks for the coffee. She smiled back and headed toward the fire fighters with the tray of cups. The soot-stained men were rolling up the hoses with slow, tired movements, the fire chief making his way among them, checking that everyone was all right.

Movement in the shadows behind the fire fighters caught my eye. A dark-haired woman, dressed in red leather from head to toe, stepped out of a darkened doorway and into the crowd near Marilyn. She took a cup of the coffee from Marilyn's tray. Then she turned, scanning the various groups, obviously looking for someone.

Her gaze lit on me and the cup stopped halfway to her lips. A look of surprise crossed her face before a current of charged heat zapped my chest like I'd been struck by invisible lightning. My magic howled and the air in my lungs turned fiery hot.

I gasped mentally, the vise grip on my lungs too tight to do it out loud. Emilia sat beside me on the bench, one hand awkwardly patting my back. Abel was still milking Liddy for attention and Cain was sitting beside me, kneading my thigh with his front paws. They didn't notice the woman or what she was doing to me.

A self-assured smile lifted the corners of her lips, erasing the momentary surprise. She raised her chin in salute, backed into the shadows and disappeared.

The lock on my lungs released the second she vanished. I sat there, stunned, trying to figure out who the woman was, why she'd saluted me like Kitanna had done and then disappeared. How she'd been able to affect my magic so strongly.

The Pyro.

She had indeed hung around to make sure the job was done.

And now she knew she'd missed, just like the Tox demon.

I drew several deep breaths, but the unease I'd felt earlier returned. I scanned the firefighters again. Most of them had removed their helmets and some had shucked their heavy turnout coats, but none of them were Adam. The fire chief walked among them, asking questions I couldn't quite hear. As he moved in and out of the shadows, though, I sensed he was searching for Adam as well.

Handing my cup to Emilia, I shifted Cain over and stood, ignoring the trembling in my legs.

"What is it, Amy?" my sister asked. She rose to stand beside me. My group of friends stopped talking and looked at me as well.

The chief finished talking to two of his firefighters and then he turned my way. The set of his face and his purposeful strides set off a series of warning bells in my head.

"Adam." I started toward the building, walking as fast as my weak legs could carry me. *Please God. Please don't let it be true.*

But I knew in every cell of my body.

Adam was gone.

CHAPTER EIGHT

"Cephiel!" I flew past the fire chief, past the hoses and firefighters who'd stopped wrapping them up and looked around. There was no use calling for Adam. Where he was, he couldn't hear me. My only hope was one of two people…Luc, who was still surrounded by his hero worshipers, or…

"Cephiel! Stop ignoring me and get your ass over here!"

The fire chief, eyeing me with apprehension at the outburst, called out as I passed him. "You can't go back there. It's a hot zone."

More like a dead zone. The air temperature dropped the moment my foot hit the sidewalk on that side of the street. A chill went up my arms, raising goose bumps. My breath puffed in front of my face, creating little white clouds as if it were a wintery night in December instead of a balmy one in June.

The smell hanging on the cold air reminded me of briny water, only bitter and acidic. A layer of mordant smoke bit into my lungs and I coughed. From the corner of my eyes, I again noticed dancing shadows where there should have been none. When I turned my head in their direction, they vanished. I could only see them from my peripheral vision. I scanned every one of them for red leather. Came up empty.

Moving further into the dark alley, my eyes adjusted to the lack of light. In every spot the fire had touched, a blue-black shimmer rose from the ashes as if the magic were still burning, still at work. A doppelganger of the real fire? An echo of the Pyro's magic? Could I get a lead on the assassin if I touched it, or would the magic's ghostly fingerprint burn me as effectively as the fire had burned my apartment?

I rounded the corner at the back of the building. Cephiel stood next to the dumpster, the day's worth of garbage from the birthday party piled high and spilling over. My guardian angel looked relieved to see me. Relieved and a little disheveled. "You're okay?"

It was definitely a question. A question that pissed me off. Of course I wasn't okay. My apartment was ashes. My possessions destroyed. My boyfriend was missing and my cats had nearly been burned alive.

Hell, I'd almost been killed twice in one day. "No, I'm not okay. I'm alive, if that's what you're asking. No thanks to you, I might add. Where the hell have you been?"

32

He took two steps toward me, his Father Leonard smile strained with patience. "You asked me to keep an eye on Mikayla, remember? And I do have other charges besides you to watch over."

I wanted to slug him. I did. Lucky for him I needed to focus on Adam. "Is Mikayla safe?"

"Both Lucifer and Gabriel are here, aren't they?"

Familiar smugness laced his tone. I opened my mouth and a bunch of pent up emotions burst out, complete with a boatload of indignation. "Where's Adam? How could you let this happen? Why didn't you save my cats? What if I had been trapped in that fire? It's magical fire! I'd be dead right now. Is this your idea of being good at your job, because in my humble opinion, you *suck* at being a guardian angel!"

With every word, I'd advanced on him. Now we stood nose to nose. Even in the shadowed, smoky alleyway, I could see his expression change from smug to nervous, the whites of his eyes more noticeable.

Suppressing my magic for the past eight months had caused my physical strength to increase tenfold. I'd sent Luc flying across my bedroom just from a simple punch to the stomach a few months back. Trust me, he'd deserved it, but my metamorphosis into the Hulk hadn't been all that helpful in my opinion. Sure I could move the living room furniture whenever I needed to vacuum under the sofa for hairballs without breaking a sweat, but now I didn't even *have* living room furniture. And okay, in all honesty, when I did, I never vacuumed under it anyway.

I mean, if I was going to get a superhero power, why couldn't it have been something really cool? Like being able to fly as fast as Superman so I could reverse the Earth's spin and turn back time? Keep Adam from going behind the building and disappearing?

Cephiel knew all about my enhanced strength, and even though the earlier poisoning had weakened me, neither he nor I knew if my strength had been fully restored. I was hyped-up enough to welcome any test to find out.

Being an incompetent angel did not make him a stupid one. He took a step back, raised his hands like shields. "Amy, I..."

There was a glimmer of guilt in his eyes. I took in his appearance again. His clerical collar was undone, his shirt untucked. And was that red lipstick on his cheek? "Exactly who were watching over, Cephiel?" My mind sidetracked back to my WA peers out front and the single one who was missing. Cephiel and Marcia had been flirting around each other for months. "Oh, my, God. My apartment was burning down and you're getting it on with *Marcia*?"

Luc shimmered into being next to me. His gaze swept over me and then Cephiel, dismissing him as if he were no more than an annoying cockroach. He took hold of my fist and turned me to face him. I hadn't even realized I'd made a fist, but suddenly I wanted to use it on both of them.

I jerked my hand out of Luc's hold. "Take me to Hell. And make it quick."

He scanned my face as if searching for the meaning of life. "What?"

"That's where Lilith lives, isn't it? In Hell? With you?"

If the Devil could blanch, he did. I swear his naturally tan face paled by at least two shades. "What does Lilith have to do with your apartment burning?"

As if he didn't know. "Your *consort*," I emphasized the word to full effect, liking the way my voice echoed in the alleyway, sounding strong instead of freaked out. "She's got Adam. She wants me, but since she's sent two assassins after me today and both failed, she's kidnapped him instead."

I looked up at the night sky and raised my voice. "A sissy move, if you ask me. Obviously Lilith's not woman enough, or demon enough, or whatever the hell she is, to face me, so instead she's sending her puny minions. How's that working out for you, bitch?"

Yes, I was losing it, but to tell the truth, losing it felt good. If I didn't give into my anger, I was going to be a miserable ball of fear. I had to focus on Lilith and make stupid, if bold, ridiculous statements, because every time I imagined Adam in Hell with her, I nearly dropped to my knees and whimpered. The thought of what she might be doing to him was too terrifying, too visceral.

I refocused my anger on the two men in front of me and locked eyes with Luc. "Let's go."

"Lilith is not my consort, Amy, nor has she been in several eons."

Eons? He was going to get picky about details now?

Un*frickin*believable. "I could care less about your relationship with her." Good thing the Lying Police weren't around or I'd be in jail for all the fibs I was telling tonight. "I just want Adam back safe and sound."

"Why would Lilith want Adam?"

Was he really that dense or just playing with me? "Because of your little love triangle back when the world began. Eons ago, remember?"

Luc studied me in the darkness. His mind nudged mine, trying to read it. He couldn't get through at the moment, maybe because my frontal lobe was in complete chaos or maybe my anger was effectively blocking him. Either way, I was glad. He didn't need to see how upset I was over him and Adam having both taken a spin on Lilith merry-go-round.

Even if it had been over several eons ago. I wasn't sure how long an eon was, but frankly, it wasn't long enough.

"Do you know how many *consorts*"—he threw the term back at me—"I have had since the beginning of time?"

Like I cared. All right, I cared, but no way was I going to let him know it. "I don't have time for a peek inside your little black book, and frankly, it doesn't matter. What matters is that I trade myself for Adam. He may have taken part in your and Lilith's party all those years ago, but he doesn't deserve to be held prisoner because of my relationship with you."

Luc continued as if I hadn't spoken. "Two, Amy. Lilith and you. There were a few minor affairs over the years, but only two true companions. You and Lilith, and I never loved Lilith. She was simply the only ally I had for a several thousand years. Loneliness sometimes makes us do stupid things. Lilith was my stupid thing."

His words hit me like a ton of bricks. I'd always known he loved me, but I never realized I was the *only* woman he'd ever loved. No wonder Lilith was having an unholy cow. She didn't consider their time together an alliance of outcasts. She was in love with Luc…

Who was in love with me.

My throat went dry and lumpy. I tried to swallow and couldn't. A sharp pressure pushed against the back of my eyeballs and I whirled away from Luc and Cephiel, closing my eyes and pressing my finger and thumb against my eyelids. *I will not cry. I will not cry.*

Breathe, Amy.

In. Out. In. Out.

Luc may have loved me, but Adam needed me. While he'd had some kind of relationship with Lilith and with Eve, Luc's connection to Lilith was the strongest and that's why she was coming after me. Adam was innocent in this scenario, and me bawling like a baby—or in this case, a broken-hearted witch—wasn't going to help him.

A solid minute passed before the tears receded and my jaw relaxed. I swallowed the lump in my throat and unclenched my still-fisted hand. When I faced Luc again, my emotions were under control. Barely-there control, but control all the same. "Can't you explain to Lilith that you and I aren't seeing each other anymore? That our relationship is done. Over?"

Nothing about Luc's expression changed. His disappointment, however, was obvious. He'd hoped his words would soften me toward him, that I'd tell him I loved him as well. I can't explain how I knew this, only that at that moment, I could read his emotions—which he keeps a tight hold on—as easily as he normally reads my mind.

He shook his head. "Even if I said those words, I'd be lying, and she'd know it."

If I hadn't still cared so damned much for Luc, my heart wouldn't have continued to thud so heavily against my ribcage. Even after eight months of separation, he loved me. He was still hanging around me, leaving his dirty banana split bowl on the table for me to clean up one minute and rescuing my cats from becoming charcoal briquettes the next.

Doesn't change anything. You can't leave Adam in the pit with Lilith. "Then I guess we better go."

"I can't take you to Hell, Amy."

"Can't or won't?"

Cephiel stepped to Luc's side. "The only way you can enter Hell is if you're dead."

That stopped me for a second. I had to die to go to Hell? Did that mean Adam was…dead? Of course, that's how it happened to most people, but in all my years with Luc, I'd never asked much about the place, or cared about the details in regards to getting in. Luc had owned my soul. I'd given it to him freely. The dying part, though, was far off into the future. A future I hadn't worried about.

Now I was facing a much sooner departure date. Like, immediately. I hadn't said goodbye to anyone. Hadn't hugged the cats one last time, or willed my possessions, what few were left, to anyone. And I wasn't sure now, when my soul was no longer bound to Lucifer, exactly where I'd end up. I needed to go to Hell to get Adam out, whether he was dead or alive, but what if I went to Heaven instead?

Don't laugh. Odds were slim, but a part of me held out a fraction of hope I'd earned my way upstairs after all these months of being a good person. Not that I thought it would be a heck of a lot of fun in Heaven, but I'd overheard a few of Gabe's stories and had a new perspective on the place. It didn't sound all that bad.

At least Lilith wasn't there.

So I stood there, shifting my weight from foot to foot and biting the inside of my cheek, my mind cart-wheeling. I didn't want to die, but what choice did I have? Lilith probably wasn't going to give up. Did I want to live with assassins dogging my every move? Eventually, one was going to get lucky, and how many of my friends would get hurt in the meantime? Could I really abandon Adam and hide from her while she destroyed everyone and everything I loved?

All I wanted at that moment was a hot shower and my bed for twelve hours of sleep. I'd have given anything to forget about all of it. I needed to clear my head and regroup, but there was no time. Lilith probably didn't sleep. Neither would her demon assassins.

I stepped forward, going toe-to-toe with Luc. Seemed like my night to get in everyone's face. "If you kill me, you can take me to Hell and make the exchange, right?"

He met my look with cool detachment.

I plunged on. "If I'm dead, I can still fight her, though, right? I mean, I'll still have a body and a mind in Hell, won't I?"

Luc and Cephiel exchanged a worried look. They both thought I'd lost my mind. Maybe I had.

"You want me to kill you, take you to Hell and let you rescue Adam."

That summed it up efficiently. "Yes."

Cephiel blustered. "You can't be serious."

He still thought he was going to save my soul from eternal damnation. "You got a better idea, Mr. Guardian Angel, who couldn't keep a flea safe?"

"He may not," Luc said. "But I do."

"Oh, yeah? And what is that?"

Luc raised one hand, laying his index and middle fingers on my forehead. My body seized up and my magic sucked wind as it plunged down a long distance as if I'd jumped off the side of a mountain. Before I could fight back, my eyes rolled up into my head and the shadows, still lurking in the dark of the moon, took me under.

CHAPTER NINE

Thud, thud, thud. A splitting headache pounded from my temples all the way to the base of my neck. For ten ticks of the grandfather clock in the corner of the room where I lay in bed, I wasn't sure where I was. Blinking, I noticed a painted skull on the clock where the sun/moon symbol was usually placed above the number twelve and a collection of vertebra on a backbone swinging in place of the normal pendulum. Hideous tribal masks hung in groupings on each wall and centered between them was an ornate picture of the African voodoo goddess Mami Wata.

Keisha's taste in decorating gave even me, a witch who'd spent her fair share of time with the occult, the shivers. She really needed to stop watching Bravo and switch to HGTV.

The clock hands pointed out it was twenty minutes after two. Two in the afternoon unless I'd been out for twenty-four hours. Afternoon sun streamed through the bedroom window, casting an eerie glow on the masks, confirming it was daytime.

Two warm lumps of cat snuggled next to me. Cain on my right, the upper half of his body lying on my chest. Abel curled in a ball on my left. Cain slit one eye open to look at me, seemed confident I wasn't going anywhere, and resumed his soft kitty snores.

One good thing about Keisha's interior design skills, she always buys mattresses with pillow tops. Gotta love a good pillow top. When you're lying in it, you can forget the Queen of Hell wants your head on a silver platter and your current- and ex-boyfriends slept with her. You can forget your stomach hurts from being poisoned and your arm has burn marks from acid nail polish. Snuggling down into that solid rectangle of comfort that molds perfectly to your tired body and aching head gives you a brief respite from the ugly facts about your life.

I closed my eyes for another minute, willing away the pain in my head and trying to remember how I'd ended up at Keisha's. My memory touched on a vague recollection of a discussion with Luc and Cephiel behind the ice cream shop and then it went blank.

Luc.

He'd touched my forehead. After that point, I couldn't remember a thing.

38

Anger flared for half a second, then went out just as fast. My body, my brain, my magic…everything was hung-over from the previous day's and night's events. I couldn't even work up righteous indignation.

Well, maybe a little. At least enough to yell at him in my mind. *Luc! What the hell did you do to me? Get your fiery ass back here! I have a few things to say to you!*

Nothing. No response. No shimmering Devil appearing next to the grandfather clock.

If I'd still been an active witch, I would have hexed him with something particularly nasty, which wouldn't have done much except piss him off, but even that would have given me a teensy bit of satisfaction. Instead all I could do was call him names.

Scaredy cat! Wuss! Chicken!

If he heard me, he chose to ignore my gibes.

Fine. He couldn't avoid me forever.

My mind stewed for a minute or two and then Adam's face popped into it. Adam. Lilith. The fire. Lilith had kidnapped Adam.

Like the previous night, my instincts and my magic knew it was fact. Her assassins had failed twice to kill me. Adam had been an easy target. She wanted me to come after him.

In my current state, that was going to be a challenge. Easier to get her to come to me. But could I just call her up?

I shrugged. Worth a try.

"Hey, Lilith. Enough with the games already. If you want me, come and get me. Just let Adam go and you can have me willingly."

Willingly was sort of an exaggeration. As soon as I was sure Adam was safe, I was going to scratch her eyes out. Or die trying.

The grandfather clock ticked the seconds by loudly. The only other sounds were my breathing and the homey clatter of pots and pans coming from downstairs. Keisha.

Cain shifted on my chest, kneading his paws against my ribcage, eyes half-mast. Making myself a target in Keisha's home wasn't my best move. She could get hurt. Cain and Abel could get hurt. I should have waited until I was back on my feet and away from everyone I cared about.

Fortunately, Lilith wasn't biting and neither were her assassins. Incompetent, really. Here I was, lying in a hot mess with little strength to defend myself, and they chose to ignore me.

A thought struck and I mentally slapped my forehead. Duh. Odds were Keisha, Luc and Cephiel had somehow quarantined me. Set up wards around Keisha's condo. I doubted very much Lilith or her minions could hear or find me if they were looking.

Which at least gave me a reprieve long enough to think.

Stroking Cain's fur, I ignored the headache while ideas pulsed inside my head along with the pounding in my temples. Finding Lilith was one thing, but once I did, how was I going to confront her?

I have a lot of confrontations in my life. My usual modis operandi is the direct route—kick-ass-and-take-names kind of directness—but the stupidity of that plan, now that I'd had some sleep, thanks to Lucifer, *the rotten sneak*, seemed obvious. Hell was her territory. She'd have the upper hand and home field advantage. I needed a better approach than to walk in with guns blazing—or in this case, my sarcastic mouth running rampant—and a well-thought out strategy to extricate Adam.

Wait. What had Luc told me last night? I couldn't go to Hell unless I was dead. Adam couldn't die twice, right? Not technically anyway. Gabriel had brought him back to a corporal state of being and returned him to Earth. Which meant Adam couldn't be in Hell.

Unless one of Lilith's assassins had killed him.

But then what good would he be as a trade?

No, he was still alive, which meant he wasn't in Hell.

At the realization, I sat up much too fast, making the room spin and the cats freak out. Cain meowed and leapt across my body, landing on Abel. Abel, in turn, hissed, stuck all his claws out and took a swing at Cain. Half a second later, both of them rolled off the bed in a tangled, mad cat ball of fur and claws.

"A little jumpy?" I said to them. I would have laughed at their comic display but my head throbbed from sitting up too fast, and I grabbed it before sliding back down into the cushiony pillow. *Slowly, Amy. Move slowly.*

One thing was for certain. As soon as I could move faster than a snail, I was going to kill Lucifer.

Over the next few minutes, I managed to sit upright. Once I was standing, things actually improved. The pounding in my head eased and the room stopped spinning. A few deep breaths, a trip to the bathroom, and I was almost good as new.

Okay, I still felt like crap, but I ignored my body's complaints and focused on my new idea. If Lilith had Adam, and my instincts and magic insisted she did, she couldn't be in Hell. She was here, in Eden, and that meant I could find her, confront her and win the day. I did a Rocky-style fist to the sky pump, and the minute I raised my fist, I did a very non-Rocky move and lost my balance, toppling back into bed.

When I finally made it downstairs half an hour later, Keisha and Gabe were in her kitchen, him sitting at the breakfast bar reading *Car & Driver* magazine. His wings were out in all their glory, but they were no longer angelic white. Over the last few months, since he'd been on Earth, they'd turned shiny platinum, dense and shadowy and much more unnerving than his once bright white ones. A side effect from falling to Earth? Or from sin?

Keisha was brewing something on the stove that smelled like chicken soup. Really delicious chicken soup with fat noodles and chunks of carrots and celery. It's hard to tell with a voodoo priestess, though. They use chickens for everything, and most of it I don't recommend eating.

At least in here the décor was (what else?) a chicken theme, but in the cute and normal kitchen-y way, not the creepy witch doctor way.

"Well, look who's up?" Keisha smiled a relieved smile, snagged a black bowl from a nearby cabinet and started filling it with the simmering concoction in front of her. "How's the stomach?"

Hunger reared its pretty little head, and I salivated as I stumbled to the breakfast bar and sat heavily on one stool. Gabe glanced at me and went back to reading about fast cars. His menacing wings rippled ever so slightly in annoyance.

"Please tell me that's homemade chicken noodle soup."

Keisha slid the bowl and a spoon in front of me and steam rose in tantalizing whiffs. While I blew on the hot liquid and slurped down spoonful after spoonful, she made herbal tea. It was a lemon-blueberry combination that went perfect with the soup. I savored every sip, every spoonful.

"Does your arm feel better?" she asked, and for the first time, I noticed the bandage on my arm was fresh. "I applied some special salve to your burns."

My forearm did feel better. A cool, comforting softness, from the salve or the cotton bandage, had replaced the stinging pain. My pounding head and thoughts about Adam and Lilith, had kept me from noticing the difference. "Thank you." I held up my arm. "Good as new."

Actually, after the soup, all of me was in better shape. Energy pulsed in my veins like I had drunk a gallon of coffee instead of a simple cup of tea. My head was clear and light without the headache weighing it down. I still needed a shower to get the smell of smoke out of my hair, and I knew from the quick glance I'd seen in the bathroom mirror during my pee run, I looked atrocious, but I felt stronger and more in control than I had in the past twenty-four hours.

Keisha handed me a business card. "Fire marshal stopped by while you were sleeping. She's investigating the fire and wants you to call her." She handed me a second business card. "This is from the detective looking into Adam's disappearance. The station fire chief was very concerned and called in the police, I guess. Mr. Detective also has some questions for you."

Both cards were made from official-looking embossed cardstock. The fire marshal's name, Natasha Anayas, was written in red, flowing Victorian script. Quite impressive for a fire marshal I thought. The detective's was in flat black no nonsense ink, which seemed more professional.

No matter. Both cards were going in the trash the minute I got up. What was I going to tell a fire marshal and a police detective? *The fire was caused by a demon and Adam was kidnapped by the Queen of Hell.*

Oh, yeah, that would land me in the fourth floor mental ward at the county medical center before the day was over.

"Emilia is quite upset that Luc deposited you here instead of at her place." A slight smile danced across Keisha's face. "Luc thought I could keep you safer than she could and she had a small temper tantrum about it. You probably should call her too."

Poor Em. Since we'd reconciled our estrangement, she'd been the ultimate big sister, trying to look out for me and protect me at every turn.

But Luc had been right to leave me in Keisha's capable hands. Emilia was a white witch walking on the side of good. Take it from me, in the real world, it takes evil to fight evil. Keisha was the odds on favorite in that department.

I ran my hands through my hair and forced myself to ask, "The apartment's totally gone, isn't it?"

Keisha's smile faded then reemerged, strained. "At least the ice cream shop is still intact."

Which made no sense. I turned the barstool to face Gabriel, fighting the numb sensation threatening to engulf me over the loss of my apartment. "Why is that? Did you put some kind of spell on it?"

Gabe's wings rippled, one long sweep from the curved arches to the tips. "I am not a witch. I do not cast spells."

No, but he was an angel. He had supernatural powers. "So, what, you put a protection *blessing* on it?"

"Wherever I dwell is consecrated ground. Evil cannot touch me."

Evil could touch him and her name was Keisha. "Uh, huh. Well, it would have been nice if your consecrating powers had extended to my apartment."

He glanced my way without making eye-contact, as if I were an annoying fly buzzing around his head. "You are evil, therefore your dwelling is evil."

Leave it to Angelzilla to call a spade a spade. "Speaking of evil, where's Luc?"

His wings moved up and down in a shrug, attention never leaving the red Ferrari on the glossy page in front of him. "I do not keep tabs on the Devil."

"You've been attached to his right hip for the past two months. You must have some idea where he is. Did he go looking for Adam and Lilith?"

Gabe tensed at the mention of Lilith. His wings froze in mid-ripple. He flipped the page, met my eyes. "I am not my brother's keeper."

Curious at his reaction, I wished I could read his mind. "What do you know about Lilith?"

"Nothing," he said a little too quickly and he would have been more believable if his gaze hadn't slid away from mine when he said it. He returned his stare to the magazine, but I could tell he wasn't seeing the black BMW displayed on the page in front of him.

What he was seeing in his mind, who knew? Nothing ever seemed to get under Gabe's skin except my smart mouth comments. I needed to know why he'd tensed up when I mentioned Lilith. Why he didn't want to answer my question.

Sensing I was a dog going after a bone, Keisha intervened. "Why don't you just call Luc? He can still hear you, can't he?"

I didn't take my eyes off of the angel, still wishing my sixth-sense or dormant x-ray vision would kick in. Where were those cool superhero powers when you needed one? "Tried calling him. No answer. I'm hoping he went to get Adam, and in that case, it's better if I don't distract him. If Lilith's making it difficult, he won't appreciate me interrupting. She's apparently sneaky and devious and wants Luc for herself. No telling what she might try. If he's not back in another hour, I'll call again."

There was no discernable change in Gabe's body, only the faintest shift in his expression. For a moment, I sat nonplussed, trying to figure him out. What was his connection to the original woman? The woman who should have been the mother of mankind, but staged a coup and got kicked out of Eden even before sin was a four letter word, according to Kitanna. The first woman God made, not from Adam's rib like her successor Eve, but from God's own hands, making her Adam's equal. That last part was according to Cephiel.

She'd rebelled and ended up Luc's consort. From Gabriel's reaction, though, I guessed there was more to the story. Gabe, who'd brought Adam back to Earth in order to wipe the slate clean and establish himself as a god, had interacted with Lilith at some point. He must have admired her rebellion. Admired her independence. Maybe had a little thing for her...

I sat back, horror and disgust mingling in equal measures. "Holy shit. You and Lilith?"

Gabe's head snapped up, eyes meeting mine, the message in them clear. He was surprised I'd guessed the truth...and from the look he gave me, he dared me—no, he double-dog dared me—to say it out loud. His wings rippled with anger and maybe the slightest bit of fear.

He didn't want Keisha to know.

Which meant he really cared about her.

"What?" Keisha asked, her gaze bouncing back and forth between us. "He and Lilith what?"

I cared about Keisha too. No way would I bring her into this, break her heart with that information. My own heart still hurt from the knowing Luc and Adam had both hooked up with Lil, the skanky bitch.

"Nothing," I said, rubbing my head. "Do you have aspirin? My head's killing me."

It wasn't a lie. My headache had returned. Gabe returned to reading his magazine and Keisha found me some pain killers. As I downed them with the last of my tea, she said, "Luc told me your theory about Lilith kidnapping Adam and taking him to her place in Hell. Are you sure?"

"Lilith wants me, one way or the other. Both the Tox demon and the Pyro failed to kill me, and Adam was an easy target last night at the fire. She saw the opportunity and took it, knowing I'd trade myself for him."

Gabriel flipped another page. "Lilith cannot walk the Earth. If Adam was indeed kidnapped, it was not by her."

News to me. It also blew my theory that Adam wasn't in Hell, that Lilith had him stashed away on Earth. Did Lucifer know all this? Of course he did. Why hadn't he told me? Boy, was I going to chew him out when he showed up again. "Why can't Lilith hang out on Earth?"

"For the same reason you cannot walk in Hell."

I glanced at Keisha. She shrugged, not understanding her boyfriend's explanation any more than I did. I gave it a shot anyway. "Hell is for the dead and Earth is for the living. So I can't go to Hell unless I'm dead and Lilith can't come up from the pit unless she's alive."

Gabe closed his eyes briefly and let out an exasperated sigh. Started reading again.

Since there was no argument, no rippling wings, I figured I'd just gotten the equivalent of a gold star. "But that means Adam can't be in Hell."

"Adam is not of this world. His body died and his soul went to Heaven. I brought him back to Earth. He has the ability to move between the worlds like I do."

Adam didn't have any supernatural powers, but being able to move between worlds like the angels was an impressive skill to have.

So he *could* be in Hell. My initial gut feeling had been spot on. But who, if not Lilith, had kidnapped him?

Another of her minion demons, no doubt. "How do demons move between Earth and Hell?"

Another sigh. "Demons do not have souls."

But Lilith did. And Luc did. Neither were demons. Lilith had been human at one time. Lucifer was an angel, albeit a fallen one. "Luc can't get back into Heaven, though, right? Can you travel to Hell?"

For the first time during the entire conversation, Gabe fully engaged, not out of anger, like he'd reacted over me mentioning his affair with Lilith, but with complete and utter astonishment.

He drew back to his full seated height, wings quivering as if hit by a shockwave, "I would never," he said, upper lip curling in a snarl, eyes glowing with scandalized intensity, "lower myself to travel to Hell."

O-*kay*, then. Guess him and Luc wouldn't be in a retirement home together in their old age, laughing it up in Hell. Too bad, in a way, since they'd been getting along so well. I sort of hated to think about Luc having no one to laugh with.

Of course, he still had Lilith.

Skank.

Once again afraid Gabe and I were going to get into it for real, Keisha raised her hands. "Boxers, back to your corners. We need to talk about Mikayla."

Mikayla. I'd forgotten about her. "Is she all right?"

"Cephiel's keeping an eye on her like you asked." Keisha came around the breakfast bar and stood next to me, facing Gabe. "But I think it's time we had a little talk about her and her powers."

She was giving Gabe the hairy eyeball. Uh, oh. That could only mean one thing.

I jumped up, ready to choke him. "What did you do to her?"

Seeming flabbergasted, he stood, wings rippling as he glared back at Keisha. "I have not touched the witch."

"But you want to, don't you?" she said.

Whoa. The way she said it made me think she was talking about something completely different than I was.

He'd obviously heard the same tone in Keisha's voice. "I would never...not like *that*," he stammered. After a deep sigh, he shook his head and lowered his wings in what looked like an angelic version of defeat. His long fingers fiddled with the edge of the magazine. "You don't understand."

It was fun watching the big guy kowtow to my best friend. He had something up his sleeve and I was glad Keisha knew it.

"You're right. We don't understand." Leaning over, I snagged the magazine and flipped it shut. "So why don't you explain it to us, Gabriel."

CHAPTER TEN

Just as Gabe opened his mouth to respond, he stiffened, head swiveling toward the living room as if someone had called his name. His eyes turned stone-like as they locked on Keisha's front door and his wings spread to their full glory.

Gabe in full Angelzilla mode is scary stuff. A chill swept over me, raising the hair on my arms.

Ding...dong. The doorbell rang, the two chords echoing inside my head so loudly, I slapped my hands over my ears. Didn't do any good. The echo continued to bounce around inside my head like a ball in a pinball game.

All my senses, in fact, went into overdrive. The lemon scent from the tea turned acidic inside my nose. The skin on my arm burned again. My magic raged inside my chest.

Like a psychic vision, I could see embryonic magic glowing a pale sunshine yellow tinged with black around the door's edges.

Mikayla.

Gabriel started to move toward the door, but I planted my hand against his chest and shoved him back. So much for evil not being able to touch him. Either he was becoming a bit evil himself, or I wasn't anymore.

And yes, my strength, both human and supernatural, had returned in full force. His back, wings and all, hit the breakfast bar and he toppled to the side.

Now that was fun.

"You take care of him," I told Keisha. "I'll handle Mikayla."

Keisha grabbed Gabe by the arm and hustled him toward the steps leading upstairs. "I've warded the whole place against everyone except the three of us. She can't come in here."

Better if she didn't anyway. Gabe was obviously a threat. "Then I'll go out."

"It's too dangerous."

I waved her off and grabbed the door handle, heat and cold arching through my hand and up my arm in a tangled helix of magical euphoria the instant I touched it.

I couldn't help myself. I drew a deep breath, half closing my eyes like Cain when I scratched the underside of his chin. "I'll be...fine."

46

Mikayla stood on the stoop in all her untainted glory. She was dressed in shorts and a t-shirt, her hair in two low pigtails again. Her hands were clasped in front of her and she was staring over her shoulder until she heard the door open.

"Hi. Remember me?" Her eyes did a quick scan and the tight smile on her lips faltered when her gaze landed on my bandaged arm. Two perpendicular creases appeared in her smooth forehead. "You're okay, right? The fire...you weren't hurt, were you? Keisha said you were fine."

My home was gone. All my belongings. My clothes, my small but dear shoe collection, my Partridge Family DVDs...even my toothbrush, toast.

At that moment, though, with Mikayla's magic drugging me and Keisha's soup energizing me, I was okay. All I had to do was keep a nascent witch from Lucifer's and Gabriel's hands and save my boyfriend from Lilith.

No biggie. "What's up, Mikayla?"

Again she glanced over her shoulder, this time in the opposite direction. "I'm sorry to bother you, but..." Her attention returned to me, the worry lines looking like a number eleven tattoo on her forehead. She lowered her voice to a soft monotone. "I think I have a...a stalker. He was in your ice cream shop yesterday, so I was hoping you might know who he was and why he's following me."

No wonder Luc hadn't answered me when I called him. "Let me guess. About so tall—" I held up a hand about a foot over my head "—blue-black hair, dark, brooding eyes, lots of smoldering bad-boy attitude and an unhealthy predilection for black clothes?"

She bit her bottom lip and shook her head. "He's got dark hair, but with gray streaks in it. Very distinguished. About your height and wearing all black, but I think he's a priest."

A small amount of relief washed over me. "Oh, that's Ceph—I mean, Father Leonard. He's not stalking you per se. He's just keeping an eye on you for me."

The eleven on her forehead disappeared as she arched her brows. "Why?"

The moment of truth. Surely she could feel the magic inside her. Surely she'd experienced some of her powers already. I wasn't certain yet exactly what she could do, but I'd bet the ice cream shop, she'd already stumbled upon them in some way, shape or form. It had probably freaked her out and she'd convinced herself she'd imagined it.

Telling someone like Mikayla she's a natural-born witch straight up with no warning is the worst thing you can do. She'd been human for eighteen years, and even if she watched *Charmed* and read Yasmine Galenorn novels, having a near-perfect stranger announce she was a witch would probably freak her out.

Yeah, I know, you're thinking, *I'd love for someone to tell me I'm a* real *witch*, but trust me, an announcement like that can cause more problems than it solves. I speak from experience.

Emilia was the one to "explain" to me that the reason I melted her Barbie Dream House when she was nine and I was seven was because I could call fire. That I was a witch.

A bad one.

Our aunt had been deep in a Jack-Daniels and occult-induced stupor for weeks and neglected to pay the light bill. Hence, we'd been playing Barbie by the light of a couple of candles. Emilia, as oldest, got her choice of dolls and left me with a few Barbie knockoffs with bad hair and even worse shoes. I'd thrown a fit and when Emilia had called me a baby, I'd felt a hot, fiery anger inside my chest. In that moment, I hated her and all the perfect Barbies in the world.

My cells tingled inside me, some crazy energy swirling around and around in circles like a tornado, growing stronger and faster when it made contact with the anger inside my chest. It felt old and dark and scared me, but it also felt powerful and...right.

Without realizing what I was doing or why I was doing it, I raised my hands and felt the anger arc from my chest out to my arms, running the length of them in a whoosh of air. A beguiling, tantalizing purpose rose from deep inside me and the flames on the candles jumped and grew twice their size.

Another burst of sensation flowed down my arms and out my hands, and a second later, the nearest flame leaned toward me, then shot straight for the plastic Barbie house. The single flame became fifty, burning the roof, engulfing the Barbies inside and melting everything the fire touched.

Emilia ran to the bathroom and came back with a cup of water. She mumbled a silly sounding rhyme, which at the time made no sense to me, and tossed the water on the fire, extinguishing it. At the same time, the anger and strange sensations coursing through my body went mute.

We stood across from each other, the scorched and half-melted house between us and both of us breathing hard. I had no idea what had just happened, but I knew it was both good and bad. I had touched something amazing inside me with my anger and it excited me as much as it scared me. As the smell of melted plastic filled the room, I looked at my big sister for help in understanding it and realized I had a whole new level of awe for her as well. Whatever was stirring in my chest, she possessed it too.

The candles continued to flicker around us and our aunt's snores echoed softly from her bedroom down the hall. But when Em finally raised her eyes and met my wide-eyed stare, her eyes were flat and hard with disappointment. Her beautiful Barbie house, the one she'd waited for years to get, was damaged beyond repair.

More than that, though, the disappointment reflected in her eyes was directed at me. "Why can't you be normal?" she'd shouted. "Why do you have to be evil? Why do you have to ruin EVERYTHING?!!?"

She'd finished off her angry tirade with one final, damaging blow. "You're the worst sister, *ever.*"

At seven years old, I believed everything my big sister told me. If she said it, it was true. When she proclaimed I wasn't normal, that I was evil, my world shifted. Instead of a powerful fiery sensation inside my chest, this time it felt stone cold. My heart and whatever else existed next to it shriveled and shrank away from her and her words.

I hid in the attic for two days after that, despite her apologies and pleas for me to come out. The cold inside my chest faded into a sort of numbness. I plotted running away and over the next few months succeeded three times, each time, my aunt finding my hiding place two blocks over at the cemetery and dragging me back home. I went to the cemetery because I could feel the dark magic there in the earth, feel it on the air currents circling the cemetery. It called to me and filled with me a weird kind of hope. Maybe I was evil, but evil was powerful. Evil accepted me.

I longed for my mother to return during those months. Not just to love me and take me away from my aunt, but to reassure me I wasn't evil. That I was normal. That the magic inside my chest was a gift, not a curse.

She didn't return. Emilia and I searched for her in our teens but never found her or our father, whom our aunt told us was dead but refused to tell us where he'd been buried. As an adult I wasn't sure the return of our mother would have set me on a different path than the self-fulfilling one I'd chosen, but I saw no point in dropping a bomb on Mikayla or any other witch coming into her powers. Better to let them figure it out themselves and then provide some guidance if necessary. Give them the choice whether to embrace good or evil.

But I didn't have months or weeks or even days to get her on board. The Devil was after her and so was a pain-in-the-ass angel. "Mikayla, we need to talk."

All emotion fell off her face, like she'd wiped the slate clean. She swallowed visibly and for one heartbeat, I thought she knew I was referring to her magic. "You're firing me, aren't you? I haven't even worked a single day yet, and you're already firing me. You can't do that. I really need this job."

Crap. This was going to be harder than I expected. "I'm not firing you, but in case you haven't noticed, the ice cream shop is closed."

"Wait, you're not firing me?" She bobbed up and down, grinning as big as the Cheshire cat, then reached out and pulled me into an embrace, forcing me to bend over since I was a few inches taller than her when she was in flip-flops.

"Oh, my God, thank you. I promise you won't regret it. I'm going to handle all the kids' birthday parties and I don't mind working nights or weekends or holidays or anything."

Gently, I pushed her back and righted myself, chuckling at her enthusiasm. "As soon as the shop's up and running again, we'll work something out, okay?"

She did another bob, pigtails bouncing against her shoulders. "The ice cream shop is fine. I drove by there on my way over. We just have to get rid of that ugly yellow tape in front of it and we're back in business!"

That ugly yellow tape was probably a Do Not Cross police tape or maybe the fire marshal had placed it there. Either way, I felt compelled to go see the shop for myself, Mikayla's enthusiasm getting to me.

Focus on the positive. I still had the shop, even if my apartment was gone.

An ancient black VW bug was snugged up next to the curb behind her. Inside on the passenger seat, a Rottweiler sat watching us. His eyes were intelligent, coat glossy and sleek. He was too big for the front seat—too big for the car, really—and it forced him to drop his head in order to see out the half-opened window. Through the crack, he stared at me.

Intense. I shivered despite the warm afternoon sun. "Is that your car?"

Mikayla nodded. "It was my granny's. She gave it to me, and I know it isn't much to look at, but I love that car. She died a few months ago, and sometimes, when I'm in the Bug, I can still feel her there, y'know?"

I had the same feeling about Evie's, which my grandmother had willed to me upon her death. I hadn't known her well—I'd spent two weeks with her one summer during high school—but sometimes I felt a connection to her that transcended life and death. "Did she give you the dog too? He's a big one."

Mikayla walked toward the car and I followed. "She. My neighbor had a family emergency out of town. Nikita's staying with me for the weekend until he gets back."

Nikita stared at me with those intense eyes. She was a beautiful Rottweiler. Didn't even pant.

But dogs were in the kid department. I thought I liked them, but I'd never had one and they made me a bit nervous. Especially big, hulking Rottweilers. Beautiful or not, they seemed…dangerous. And not in an evil way.

Evil I can handle. Giant dogs with extra-large teeth, no thanks.

Nikita probably liked hanging with Mikayla, going for rides in her VW. Mikayla was obviously a good person, destined to become a good witch. Maybe I didn't need Cephiel watching her back. Maybe I should just butt out and let whatever happened happen.

Until I knew for certain what Gabriel was planning and that Luc couldn't touch her soul in exchange for mine, though, I wasn't leaving her alone. "Why don't we drive over to the shop and have a look at the damage?"

"Why don't we," she echoed and skipped around to the driver's side.

The condo's door opened behind us. Keisha stuck her head out and gave me her impatient face. "What are you doing?"

"Heading over to check on the shop. I need to see how much damage there might be."

She opened the door all the way and made a discreet motion for me to come talk to her. I turned to Mikayla and nodded my head in Keisha's direction. "I'll be right back."

"I'll move Nikki into the back seat."

Good luck with that. Nikita wasn't going to fit in the VW's back seat any better than she did in the passenger seat. She was probably going to hate me for making her give up shotgun.

On the front stoop, Keisha set her hands on her hips and started in on me before I could open my mouth. "You can't go to the shop. One of those assassins might be waiting for you to show up. It's not safe. Luc said you should stay here until he returned."

"Yeah, well, Luc isn't answering my calls, and Gabe said the shop was structurally protected by his angel mojo. As long as I'm inside, doors locked, and no one's there with me besides Mikayla, what could possible happen?"

Keisha is my best friend for a reason. Along with her love for expensive shoes and decadent ice cream concoctions, she's just as bullheaded as I am. We argued for another minute, and she glared red-hot laser beams at me, but I stuck to what passed for logic. If the ice cream shop could survive magical fire, it could survive anything. And I'd be perfectly safe inside.

Keisha agreed with my logic, but refused to budge on principal. Finally, I said, "Why don't you just come with us? You can add a ward or two to the place for extra protection."

Her priestess bluster deflated a smidge. She took a deep breath, straightened her spine in an Angelizza move, which only put her a half an inch taller than me, and raised her chin. "Fine. I will." She shook a gold skull-ringed index finger in my face. "But I'm warning you, this is a bad idea."

Wouldn't be my first bad idea. Nor would it be my last...unless, of course, one of Lilith's assassins made good on her contract. Still, I couldn't live forever inside Keisha's condo. I had to figure out a way to confront the problem, and it continued to seem like I would have to die, go to Hell and rescue Adam. "Have you ever brought anyone back from the dead?"

Keisha's beautiful smooth dark skin turned an ashen gray. "What in Mami Wata's name are you talking about?"

"You summon spirits all the time. I thought maybe, you might know how to go a step farther, and not only bring their spirit back, but their body also."

The ringed finger pointed at me again. "You are up to no good, aren't you?"

Yes, yes I was. This idea, like my earlier one about Adam not being in Hell, took root and continued to grow. Between Keisha, Gabriel, Luc and Cephiel, someone had the power to kill me, take me to Hell, and then bring me back. Adam, too. All I had to do was convince the right person or team of people to give it a try. "The longer we stand out here in the open, the better my chances of getting killed by an assassin."

Keisha sighed. "I'll get my keys to the shop and Gabe and I will follow you there."

"No Gabe. Not while Mikayla's around."

"I'll control Gabe." She gave me a set look and I knew she meant it. "You're the one I'm worried about."

I was worried about me too. It wasn't every day I planned my own death and possible resurrection. "I have to get Adam back, Keisha. If Luc and Gabe won't help, I have no choice but to confront Lilith on my own. She won't stop coming after me until I'm dead anyway, so I'm going to need all the help I can get."

Little did I know how true my words would turn out to be.

CHAPTER ELEVEN

The ice cream shop was exactly the way I'd last seen it, the exception being the party mess had been cleaned up.

The black and white checkerboard floors gleamed. The red and white booths were clean, the silver napkin holders pushed up against the walls and properly filled with white napkins just the way I liked them. The chairs and tables rounding out the seating options stood in their snug little groupings, waiting for a new day of customers. And the framed pictures on the walls hung straight.

Behind the counter, scoops were laid out in surgical precision, white cleaning towels were washed, dried and folded in neat piles. The motors under the ice cream displays hummed softly, reassuring me all was okay.

The faintest scent of smoke hung in the air, so faint in fact, I might have imagined it. As I walked around touching everything to reinforce it was indeed real and not an illusion, I simply couldn't believe the fire that had ravaged my apartment to ashes hadn't harmed a single thing inside Evie's.

For once, I said a heart-felt prayer of gratitude to The Big Guy in the sky. It was such a relief to walk in and see everything normal, I nearly did a Mikayla-inspired skip across the floor. The assassin had stolen more than my possessions. She'd stolen the innate safety I'd always felt inside this building, and she'd almost stolen the connection with my grandmother who'd I'd barely known before she passed and willed the shop to me.

Covering all the bases, I sent up a mental thanks to the Universe, Fate, Buddha and every other deity I could remember...which was an extremely short list, but what do you expect from an ex-witch who previously only worshipped the Devil?

While I was at it, I tossed a thank you his way, too, once again for rescuing my cats. I couldn't imagine waking up without their soft little bodies nestled next to me every morning.

Of course, if I didn't stop Lilith, I wouldn't be waking up, period.

Keisha and Mikayla stood near the cash register, talking in soft tones while Keisha kept an eye on me. Gabriel, wings heavily glamored by one of Keisha's spells so Mikayla couldn't see them, helped himself to his latest ice cream jones—chocolate cherry brownie supreme. He dug out two heaping scoops and slapped them into a bowl, all the while pretending he wasn't paying attention to Mikayla or Keisha.

I knew better. His movements were drawn out and purposeful, as if he were forcing himself to create the illusion of casual when in reality he was so hopped up on being that close to Mikayla, his hands shook.

Besides the fact he was playing Mr. Cool, he was eating the last of my current favorite ice cream. Kind of freaked me out Gabe and I currently had the same taste in ice cream. I mean, he's so *not* chocolate when it comes to ice cream. He's definitely pure vanilla. The kind with actual vanilla bean speckles dotting through the white cream. At the very most, Gabe might be a vanilla fudge swirl, but he's not dark cherries, rick dark chocolate and brownie chunks.

"Leave some for the customers," I growled at him. What I really meant was, *leave some for me, you scrounging, ungrateful Jolly White Giant.*

Sending me a look that made me think he knew exactly what my Amy-speak meant, he tossed the dirty ice cream scoop in the sink, challenging me with his gaze, and left it there for me to wash.

Like I said, ungrateful.

His presence, however, had saved Evie's. Not that he'd done it intentionally, but I had to cut him slack anyway. I headed for my office.

My hand on the doorknob, I paused as Mikayla called from behind me, "Can I bring Nikita in? I don't like leaving her in the car when it's this hot, and she's really well-behaved."

I started to utter the no animals rule and point toward the sign clearly posted on the front door. But when I looked at Mikayla, she was giving me her innocent, *I'm a great person and a responsible dogsitter* look, and my normal staunchness wavered. If I said no, she'd probably leave, and we still hadn't had The Talk yet. "Bring her around back. I'll let you in through the outside office door."

She did that bob up and down thing like she had springs in her shoes and clapped her hands together. Her magic also responded and seemed to hug me from across the room. "Thank you, Amy!"

No matter what Luc said about getting her soul in exchange for mine, she was not going to Hell. I wouldn't allow it.

My office was the way I'd left it as well. The only thing missing was the vase of flowers. Good riddance to that. The memory of the previous day's illness made me queasy. Shaking off the memory, I unlocked the door to the alley, caressed the edge of my desk and sank into my chair. A sense of relief flooded my chest and I leaned in the chair and closed my eyes, pretending for a moment everything was normal again.

"Amy."

Luc's voice shredded my daydream and I jerked upright. As usual, he was drop dead gorgeous and my magic as well as my heart did a little dippy-do inside my chest.

Today, he wore a short-sleeved silk t-shirt that allowed me to see the barest outline of his six-pack. If I hadn't been so upset about him putting me down for the count, I might have drooled.

He stood on the other side of my desk at a respectable distance. Too scared to stand in range of my fists, no doubt.

"What the hell did you do to me last night?" I said, proud of the fact my voice didn't squeak and give me away. "I ended up sleeping for nearly twelve hours and woke up to a monster of a headache. Whatever that was, don't ever do that to me again."

No emotion crossed his face. "You were hysterical. Drastic action was necessary."

Hysterical? There was a word I hated, especially when applied to me. I might have been emotional after watching my apartment go up in flames and realizing my boyfriend had been kidnapped, but hysterical?

I took a deep breath to keep from jumping the desk and going for his jugular. "Where have you been? Didn't you hear me calling you earlier today? Why didn't you tell me Lilith couldn't walk around up here and that Adam could only go to Hell if he was dead?"

His face remained a total mask, controlled and hiding all emotion. For a brief second, I wondered why he was camouflaging his emotions. Then he said, "I went to see Lilith," and I forgot all about his forced pretense.

I came out of my chair. "Is Adam okay?"

Luc flicked his gaze to my bandaged arm, back to my face. "I can heal that for you."

My heart stuttered. Not because Luc healing my arm would be a rush of pure pleasure, but because he'd avoided answering my question. I sat back down. "Tell me he's not dead. Tell me she's not torturing him."

Something flashed in his dark eyes. He took a step toward the desk. "He's not dead, but he is in Hell with her. She's not torturing him…much."

Much? A lump formed in my throat. Lilith wasn't just a skank, she was a bona fide psycho. I swallowed the lump and stood again, digging my fingertips into the desk so hard it hurt. "Why didn't you rescue him?"

"She would only have one of her…employees…kidnap him again. Unless he returns to Heaven, he won't be safe from her."

The thought of Adam heading back to Heaven caused havoc in my heart. My options were wide open now, weren't they? Leave him in Hell to suffer at Lilith's hands, or bust him out and end his second chance at life—a life he was particularly proud of—here on Earth. Force him to trade in Sin City Chocolate ice cream, his favorite, for milk and honey.

I tapped the desk with my index finger. "Go back down there and get him. Cephiel can put him on the train bound for Heaven as soon as you return."

"He doesn't want that."

"How do you know what he wants?"

"He told me."

Oh. "You talked to him?"

"Eve is also Lilith's prisoner. Adam won't leave without her, but he does not want you interfering in any way."

Lucifer paused, waiting probably for me to argue, but I was speechless. "He doesn't want to return to Heaven and he's willing to endure Lilith's cruelty until he can figure out how to destroy her and return to Earth. With Eve."

The lump was back in my throat, pressing against my esophagus like I'd swallowed a dozen marbles. Did that mean Adam wanted Eve instead of me or was this simply part of his hero make-up? Hurt, anger, boiled inside my chest. Along with fear for him. I bit it all back. "Can he? Destroy Lilith?"

One of Luc's brows twitched and a muscle jumped in his jaw. "Odds are not in his favor."

"Then you do it. Force her to give up Adam, and Eve, too, I guess. Kick Lilith out of Hell." I slammed my hand down on the desk. "Or destroy her."

He looked like he wanted to step closer, but held back, glancing at my fist still on the desk. "Amy, Lilith isn't what you think…"

The alley door opened and Mikayla walked in, Nikita beside her on a leash. "Oh," she said, pulling up short at the sight of Luc. Her mouth hung open for a second and then she stammered, "Am I…uh…interrupting?"

Nikita whined softly. Rubbing my fingers against my temples more out of frustration than pain, I shook my head. Luc was about to tell me I didn't understand Lilith's great powers or something close to that, and give me some lame-ass excuse about why he couldn't march back down there and destroy her. I didn't want to hear it. I'd been right from the start. The only way to stop Lilith was to trade myself for Adam. This was between me and the Queen of Hell. "Come on in, Mikayla. Just don't let the dog go into the ice cream shop."

Mikayla smiled demurely at Luc and started to slip past him, but Nikita stood glued to the floor, and since she appeared to outweigh Mikayla by a good thirty pounds, Mikayla pulled up short once more. "Nikita, heel."

Nikita didn't like Luc, that was obvious. Smart dog.

I circled the desk and gave her a pat on the head like the dog and I were suddenly the best of friends, mentally telling Luc to take a hike. Nikita leaned into my legs and accepted my head strokes, seemingly happy at our newfound friendship as well.

Luc reluctantly sidled a few steps to his right, clearing a wide space between him and the dog. As he did so, I didn't miss the eye roll he shot at the ceiling of my office.

In case you don't know, the Devil hates being interrupted.

Bully for him. I hated having my world turned into a three-ring circus, courtesy of his skanky, psycho consort.

Mikayla continued to tug on Nikita's leash, but the dog stayed attached to my leg. Poor thing. She was probably scared of him. After all, Luc put the "d" in danger.

Cain and Abel were going to turn their noses up at me the second they got a whiff of Nikita on my pants. While I hated to leave her, it appeared Luc wasn't taking the hint to clear out. "I'm going upstairs to check out the damage," I said, giving Nikita's head a parting pat. At the same time, I gave Luc an empathic glare. "Why don't you come with me?"

I didn't want to hear more about Lilith, but if I was going to take her on, it seemed prudent to get the whole story. I gestured for him to lead the way and he acquiesced, opening the inside door and heading for the hallway.

Unfortunately, Nikita was not about to let me leave her behind. As Luc and I headed toward the stairs leading up to what had been my second-story apartment, Nikita dragged Mikayla behind us.

"Mikayla, you have to take her back to the office."

"I know." She yanked on the leash with no effect. "I'm trying."

Nikita stared up at me with pleading eyes. I called for Keisha. She and Gabe appeared, Gabe still sucking down my ice cream. "Help Mikayla get the dog back in my office."

Keisha gave me one of her, *what do I look like, the hired help* faces, and Gabe fluttered his wings, giving off a similar amount of indignation.

Dogs liked treats, right? I pointed at Gabe. "Tempt her with some ice cream and lead her back to the office."

Gabe dropped his spoon in the bowl and looked at me like I'd suggested he stop having voodoo sex with Keisha.

Mikayla frowned. "I don't think ice cream is good for dogs."

Ice cream is good for everyone, animals included. The Food Pyramid should include a scoop of any flavor in its daily recommended diet. "It's organic, how bad can it be?"

Nikita seemed to realize we were talking about her. She eyed Gabe's bowl. "Try it," I said, liking the dog even more. "A few licks of the stuff won't kill her."

Keisha tried to take Gabe's bowl and spoon, but he lifted it over his head, way out of her reach.

"Fine." She turned on her heel. "I'll get some vanilla for her."

A minute later, she returned with the promised vanilla, holding a spoonful of it out to the Rottweiler. The dog took a few wary steps, nose wiggling as she caught the scent and tongue licking her generous chops before she'd even tried it. Keisha let her have a taste, then began backing toward the office. I gave Luc, who was on the first stair step a push. "Let's go."

"Where are you going?" Keisha said in a low, but demanding tone. She wanted to raise her voice, I could tell, but she also didn't want to scare off the dog.

I glanced over my shoulder. "To my apart—" I caught myself, shook my head. "To the roof. I want to see if there's anything left."

Keisha glanced up from feeding the dog and opened her mouth to yell at me. I cut her off. "Don't worry. I'll be safe with Luc and…" I pointed at Gabe. "Gabriel, here, is going to earn his keep and come with us."

Gabe closed his eyes in that way of his, suggesting he was good and tired of me. Keisha, however, arched one brow at him, and suddenly he was all business, striding toward the stairs and making shooing motions with his free hand. "Fine. Go."

We hadn't even cleared the top step when Nikita howled and bounded up the stairs. Once more, she leaned on my leg, and when Luc looked down at her and frowned, she lifted the edge of one lip to show her canine teeth and growled ever so slightly.

I patted her head. "Good dog, Nikita."

CHAPTER TWELVE

My apartment had been reduced to ashes, and even in the late afternoon sun, the ashes glowed.

Soft yellow beams of sunlight filtered over the roof, which was now a story lower. Before the fire, my building had boasted the highest profile in downtown Eden and Adam and I often sat on the roof in the evenings or early mornings, soaking up the view of both the town below us and the sky above us.

Sunrises, sunsets, starry nights, full moons, even once a partial solar eclipse, they'd all been beautiful. Now, my building was the shortest one, and the towering structures nearby blocked those views, throwing pencil-thin shadows across my face as I walked around my no longer existent apartment.

Where the shadows fell over the ruins, a soft fluorescent blue outlined individual ashes. In the yellow glow of the sinking sun, the color turned a sickly green. My friends all stood a good distance away, giving me a few moments to soak it all in. Keisha and Luc were on guard, scanning the windows and rooflines around us, looking for assassins, I assumed. Gabe concentrated on his ice cream and Mikayla paced around him, biting her bottom lip and checking her cell phone for messages. Nikita padded quietly by my side, her brown paws turning a dusty grey-blue.

In my mind, I saw the rooms that had been there less than twenty-four hours earlier. Here and there, I bent down and brushed ash aside, hoping I might find something left of my furniture, my belongings. I stared at the various piles of glowing ashes and wondered, had this been my bed? Was that pile over there my favorite chair? What about this concentration of ashes? My bookcase?

Every time my fingers touched the ashes, a zap of left-over magic traced its way up my arms. The Pyro demon hadn't cared about leaving traces of her magic behind. Just the opposite. She was proud of her work and had purposely left her calling card.

I'm embarrassed to admit grief hit me like a twenty-five gallon bucket of frozen ice cream. I went down on both knees, tears overflowing my eyes no matter how hard I beat them back. Hands on my thighs, I hung my head and cried, not just over the total destruction of my possessions but over Adam too. What was Lilith doing to him? Why hadn't I considered how far she might go to get to me? How was I ever going to right this wrong?

59

I'd love to tell you my crying jag was eloquent, filled with beautifully tragic tears, but I'd be lying. I sobbed, my face turned hot, so I knew it was bright red. Snot was involved, and while it was tragic, it was in no way beautiful.

Have you ever thrown a bunch of necklaces in a drawer and then when you went to get one out to wear, the chains were all tangled and knotted up? That's how my brain felt. Like a giant ball of twisted, knotted thoughts and ideas, and no matter how I worked to untangle them, they tightened and clumped together even more. The Tox demon's words, when she was pretending to be Cephiel, echoed in my brain.

… *if you weren't so busy being a smartass all the time, you might actually be more than a washed-up witch, running a failing ice cream parlor in a rinky-dink town in the Midwest.*

Washed up, and now, it seemed, burned out as well. A complete failure. That was me.

How did humans do it? Live this way? Without magic to counterbalance the crap life tossed at them?

Of course, my current pile of crap was courtesy of magic, so I couldn't justify throwing my oath out the window in a fit of depression or rage or revenge.

And yet, without my magic, what was I?

Oh, right. A complete failure.

Luc's power tingled against my skin a second before I heard the *swish, swish* of his boots in the ashes on my left. For once I didn't fight it or reflect it. I let his supernatural energy wrap itself around me, warming me. Allowed my magic to reach for him in return and curl into his protective comfort.

He knelt beside me, silent, saving the *look on the bright side speech*, thank goodness, and simply rubbing my back with one of his strong, confident hands. A slow and gentle caress, it was full of support and love and reminded me of our times together when he'd wiped a bad day away or eased one of my stupid Amy moments with a simple caress of his hand.

Which made me cry even harder.

How was it I could be in love with two men at the same time? Not men, even. One a fallen angel and one the father of all mankind who'd returned to Earth. Extraordinary beings, both had gone to great lengths to be with me. Both continued to protect me and fight for me.

Luc's powerful hands gripped my shoulders and slowly lifted me to face him. He shifted his weight awkwardly, my tears making him uncomfortable. "All is not lost, Amy."

In his defense, I never cry. I get angry. I get even. And I often lash out unjustly—one of my many character flaws—but I don't cry when things go wrong. Ever.

I sucked in a deep, hitchy breath, lifted my face, and wiped the tears off my cheeks. I may have been a washed-up, burned-out witch, but one of my other character flaws is that I never give up. You pick a fight with me, you better be ready to fight to the death.

"With or without your help, I'm going to Hell to free Adam and kill Lilith."

"Kill her?" Luc gave me a patient smile. "You can't kill Lilith any more than you can kill me or Gabriel or Cephiel. We aren't human."

I glanced over to make sure Mikayla couldn't hear us. She was far enough away I didn't think she could hear our conversation, and busy talking to someone on her phone, but I dragged Luc several more feet to the side and lowered my voice anyway. "Lilith was human at one time and she has a soul. Gabriel told me that's why she can't walk the Earth. Because she was human and her soul was condemned to Hell when she died."

The sun continued its descent, throwing a mix of light and shadows across Luc's face. "She does have a soul, but there's more to her than what Gabriel has told you. The point is you can't kill her. Her soul is what lives in Hell, and no one but God can destroy a soul."

The maddening knot in my brain tightened further, but unless I was a complete moron, there appeared to be only one solution. "If I let the Pyro kill me, will Lilith let Adam go?"

Luc's face hardened into a dozen different planes of *don't even go there.* "Give me until morning to figure out a plan before you do anything…rash."

What he wanted to say was, *don't do anything stupid.* I appreciated his restraint. Calling me stupid never goes over well, and he'd already called me hysterical. "Adam is being tortured this very minute. I'm not waiting until morning to rescue him."

"Adam is stronger and more clever than you give him credit for. He survived Lilith's manipulation and treachery in the beginning and he will survive it now as well." Luc wiped a stray tear from the corner of my eye. "If you trade yourself for him, he'll do something equally stupid, and it will be all *Romeo and Juliet* and you'll both be dead but your souls won't end up together for eternity. Trust me."

I knew it. "So what you're saying is that I'm going to Hell, even though I've given up being a bad witch."

Luc dropped his hands. "Just give me until morning to resolve all of this. Please."

I glanced at Keisha and Mikayla, who watched us intently. "Are my friends and Emilia in danger from the Pyro?"

"All of you should stay in the ice cream shop tonight under Gabriel's care."

Having finished his ice cream, Gabriel had sat down on the edge of the building and was cleaning his fingernails with the handle of the plastic spoon. I sincerely doubted he cared one iota for me. "Great. A sleepover. We'll pop popcorn and tell ghost stories. Maybe Keisha can perform a séance."

Luc tilted his head slightly, a rather perplexed look on his face. He probably had no idea what went on at girl's sleepovers. Honestly, I was just going off what I'd seen on TV. I'd never had one or been invited to one in my entire life.

What? I'm a complete loser, remember? I could count my childhood friends on one hand. One pinkie, actually.

Leaning over, Luc kissed my forehead like I was an insolent child. "Stay inside and don't go near the doors or windows until I get back, okay?"

Even though I was no child, insolence was definitely abundant in my attitude. "Mikayla will have to stay, too, and I can't have her near Gabe."

Luc turned pensive. "You do know why he wants her clean power, don't you?"

Again, I made sure we were out of earshot. That she wasn't paying attention to us. She'd put her phone away and was staring at the skyline, lost in her own thoughts. "No. Why?"

Out of the corner of his eye, Luc shot a glance at Keisha. "He doesn't want to return to Heaven. He wants to stay here on Earth."

"He's already here on Earth."

"But he can't stay here much longer without God's permission or he'll be damned like I am. He's been given until the full moon to make his decision."

"What does that have to do with Mikayla's magic?"

"If he can possess her magic, he can also possess her body. He can, in essence, trade vessels with her. Become human."

Holy crap. "Human possession?"

Luc nodded.

"That can't be it. He'd be a girl then. Gabe's a freak, but he's an alpha male freak all the way."

"Nascent witches are extremely rare these days. He either takes Mikayla or risks certain damnation."

"Why can't he just go back to Heaven where he belongs?"

"God will strip his station as archangel for what he's done. He'd rather avoid that. Besides, he likes it down here a little too much."

Part of that was my fault. I'd made it entirely too easy for him to have his cake—or in this case, ice cream—and eat it too.

"I have to go." Luc stepped back. "Remember, stay inside the shop until I return."

Before I could stop him, he shimmered out of sight.

Mikayla stumbled over to me, her finger pointing at the spot Luc had disappeared from and her mouth moving but no sound coming out. Finally she said, "Oh, my god. Did he just…just…"

"Yep. He did." I patted her hand and steered her toward the gaping hole where the steps led back down to the shop. "We still need to have that talk."

Her lips moved again in speechless wonder. I hoped I could ease her into the magic discovery, but I didn't have a lot of energy left to be savvy. She was getting a dish of caramel macchiato and the flat out truth.

We'd only gone three steps when I realized Nikita wasn't by my side. I looked over my shoulder and saw her pawing at some ashes. "What is it, girl?"

I thought she was digging something out. As I approached, though, it seemed like she was covering something up. I tried to coax her to move over so I could see what she was pawing at, but she refused to budge. Although she didn't growl, she did keep her head lowered.

I wasn't up on dog body language, but her posture told me in no uncertain terms to back the hell off.

That would have been the smart thing to do, but as I was about to act disinterested and try to distract her so Keisha or Mikayla could recover whatever was hiding under the blue-green ashes, I spotted a sliver of white paper.

Sure my eyes were playing tricks on me, I blinked, and when it didn't disappear, I shoved ash out of the way with the toe of my foot without even thinking about Nikita's defensive body posture.

A business card, much like the ones Keisha had handed me earlier, rose to the surface. Completely undamaged and not smudge of ash anywhere on it, even though it had been buried by Nikita's pawing.

She whined as I bent and snatched it up but made no move against me. A flowing, curlicue script in fire engine red cut across the white card. Natasha Anayas. The fire marshal. Had she been up here earlier today and dropped it?

Nikita whined again and pushed her wide forehead against my leg as if urging me toward the stairs. At the same moment, the hair on the back of my neck rose to attention and my magic froze in my chest. The sensation of being watched came next and I scanned the windows and rooflines towering over me.

Hello, sitting duck.

"Everybody downstairs!" I yelled, running for the stairwell. Passing Mikayla, I grabbed her arm and jerked her with me. "Come on."

We hadn't gone three feet before all hell broke loose.

As if we'd been hit by a biblical plague, all around us, from every direction, balls of fire as big as basketballs rained down.

CHAPTER THIRTEEN

Running would have been a good idea except for the fact the Pyro liked playing supernatural dodge ball and was good at it.

At the middle school Emilia and I attended while living with our aunt, dodge ball was called Kill and the students took it seriously. The way balls flew with enough force to give you a concussion if you were unfortunate enough to get hit in the head was one thing. The way my peers' eyes gleamed with menace while unleashing their inner dark sides was another. You would have thought it was hand-to-hand combat, last man standing lives. As if all of us were soldiers instead of pimply, pubescent seventh graders.

Incidentally, I wasn't pimply, but I wasn't particularly swift or coordinated either back then, nor did I find it fun to jump around and lob balls at other people while yelling, "Kill!" at the top of my lungs. Not surprisingly, I'm not any more coordinated now, even though I was at that moment significantly more motivated to evade the "kill" since it meant being fried.

I have to hand it to Mikayla. After her first initial scream, she settled into duck, cover and evade mode, no questions asked. That's what happens in a crisis, I guess. Survival first, questions later.

Still, I couldn't help wondering what had gone wrong with Keisha's protection wards and Gabe's inherent protective presence. I also wondered where my guardian angel was.

Oh, right. Marcia needed his attention.

Three times, Mikayla and I attempted to get to the stairs. Three times we met a wall of flame, cutting off our path.

Over the sound of the fire bombs, sputtering and cracking flames, I heard Keisha shouting my name, but I couldn't see her or Gabe. Dozens of fires lit the rooftop and smoke swirled and shifted like a ghostly cloud overhead.

Mikayla coughed and said in a clearly perplexed voice, "Nikita?"

I waved smoke away from my face and glanced in the direction Mikayla was staring. Fire ran in a straight line off to our right. It connected with a second thin line running along our left and forming a point. At the head of the point stood the woman in red leather.

The red script of the fire marshal's business card flashed in my mind. Natasha. The Pyro.

Head slung low and teeth bared, Nikita moved in and out of the smoke, sneaking up behind her.

Crap. That's what I needed. The dog to get hurt while trying to defend me and Mikayla.

Natasha waved one hand and the smoke closest to us lifted on a warm breeze. She hadn't noticed Nikita slowly, step-by-careful-step advancing on her. Her hair danced like the fire, and glancing around, I noticed two important things. One, Keisha was trapped inside a circle of fire, and two, the lines of fire surrounding me and Mikayla formed a shape. An interesting shape that held us prisoner on all sides.

An inverted pentagram.

Of less importance was the fact Gabe watched from the edge of the roof, any concern for the three of us masked behind blatant irritation at all the commotion.

If I'd still been practicing dark magic, or any magic for that matter, I would have turned the fire against its host. Once more, I wondered how humans managed without magic. Then again, how often did they face down a demon?

While my commitment to my oath wavered, I sucked up my courage, coughed a few times from the leftover smoke in my lungs, and tried the first normal, human thing that came to mind.

Talking.

"You don't need all the dramatics," I said to Natasha. "Don't hurt my friends and I'll go willingly."

For a second, she looked surprised. Then suspicious. I crossed a finger over my heart and she smiled a big, happy smile, raised both hands in the air and did a double fist pump. Talk about gullible.

Nikita was only a short leap behind her now, but she was so fixated on me, she still hadn't noticed. "Yes! I did it. I did it. I'm going to get the bounty on…"

Her words ended in a surprised, "am-mrrmphh" as Gabriel, who'd apparently decided he'd had enough, said something that sounded like "cataracta" and the heavens opened above us and a giant, twilight-bespeckled waterfall rushed down, drenching us and the fires.

I thought manna was the technical "fall from heaven" substance, although I wasn't sure what manna even was, and I had serious doubts cataracts had anything to do with waterfalls, but maybe that was another one of the Latin terms Gabriel liked to sling around.

We all stood there for a second, dazed and soaked to the bone, with the exception of Gabe who was still dry and bored. Nikita was the first to move, shaking her fur and sending huge arcs of water spraying in all directions, but mostly, it seemed over Natasha.

Natasha sputtered, cursed under her breath and flung water from the tips of her fingers. She raised her gaze to mine and everyone else looked at me too. Seemed like I should say something, but I wasn't sure exactly what.

And then, like usual, I opened my mouth and sarcasm came to my rescue. I held out my arms in mock surrender. "Wanna try again? They say three times's the charm."

Natasha narrowed her eyes, and I swear, she growled under her breath. At first I thought it was Nikita, but no, it was the demon.

Good. I wanted her angry. As angry as I was. "I had planned to let you get me this round, take me to Lilith, but the fact is, when I face her, it will be on my own terms, not because some demon assassin cuts my life short."

Natasha raised a hand and a magic flame ignited on the tip of her fingers. Apparently Gabriel's waterfall hadn't extinguished her inner fire.

I really should have shut up at that point and got my butt back downstairs where I'd be safe, but blame my lack of moral fiber, I had to get in one more jab. Four times in the past two days, a demon had tried to kill me and all four times I'd made it out alive. I was feeling a bit cocky about my ability for self-preservation and I was damned tired of demons. "Hey, don't feel bad. That Tox demon. Kitanna Ivey? She failed twice yesterday, too, and I hear she's the best." I gave Natasha a goading smile. "She did have a lot more finesse, I have to say. Only the second time she failed, I sent her back to Hell, where she belongs, so you might want to reconsider what you're about to do."

"Kitanna was my *sister*." Natasha spit the word, her face turning beat red, the flame on her fingertips flashing and growing bigger.

Uh, oh. A thousand pinpricks of hot energy raced over my skin as magic arced across the space between us. My heart seized in my chest, like it had the night before, and my chest locked up.

This time, however, I wasn't paralyzed by her magic.

The flame at her fingertips sparkled hot and blue-tinged around the edges, and I had the good sense to grab Mikayla's arm and duck a split second before she let it fly.

What I'd told her was true. In those minutes when the pentagram fire imprisoned Mikayla and me, I'd decided I didn't want to die. Yes, I had to rescue Adam, but I would be smart about confronting Lilith. Giving up my life wasn't smart. In fact, that would give Lilith exactly what she wanted with no guarantee she would actually release Adam, and no way was I going to play into her manipulation.

Team player, I am not.

Natasha's fireball whizzed past my left ear, clipping a few strands of my hair and setting them on fire. I screamed like a girl—hey, you would, too, if you're hair caught on fire—and grabbed a handful of wet, sooty ashes that I slapped against my head.

A second, bigger, fire ball screamed through the night air, Mikayla and I, ground zero. Ducking wasn't going to work this time, so I threw my body in front of Mikayla like a shield and flung one hand in the air on instinct, turning my head away and hoping for the best. My magic roared and the prison I kept it in dissolved like grains of sand, sending it into my left arm.

But before it could react to the fire ball, a strange sensation rocketed through my body, starting in my right hand that was still on Mikayla's arm and shooting up my arm. The sensation felt like a rush of cold water, and as it crossed through my shoulders and chest, I cried out. It hit my heart and I shuddered as if ice cubes had been dumped down my back, my magic going suddenly, eerily silent. The water sensation rushed across my left arm and into my raised hand.

Heat from the fire ball scorched my hand, but the cold water sensation repelled it almost immediately, flowing swiftly into my fingers and blocking the fire from doing more damage. Not understanding, I glanced up and saw the fire ball speeding its way back to Natasha. Her eyes widened right before it hit her and *bam*!

The Pyro exploded in a brilliant flash of red and yellow fireworks. They shot up, up, up into the dark night sky before, one by one, winking out.

Stunned, I collapsed onto the roof, letting go of Mikayla. The cold, watery sensation evaporated as quickly as it had come, but my magic, as well as my body, felt the lingering, drenched effect. While I mentally asked myself what had just happened, a part of me already knew. I'd used magic to repel the fire ball. Only it wasn't *my* magic.

I'm an air witch for all intents and purposes. I can call fire, but I've never been able to repel it, because fire needs air to burn. On its own, air magic coils and twists and lifts me up as if I'm riding an air stream. It never, ever feels like water.

Mikayla had used her magic to save me. To save us. Her magic had overridden mine and sent the fire ball to kill Natasha.

Pretty damned impressive for a nascent witch.

The sun was completely gone now and without Natasha's fires illuminating the rooftop, it was dark as sin. Smoke still hung in wisps. I could barely make out the shapes of Keisha and Gabe and I couldn't see Nikita at all. Her black and brown fur blended in completely with the surrounding darkness.

The one thing I could see was Gabriel's white bowl. It rose from the ground and bobbed across the roof like a spectral image.

Keisha, who I could hear breathing as hard as me and Mikayla, said, "And where do you think you're going?" in Gabe's direction.

"Ice cream," he replied, the tone of his voice suggesting it was a dumb question.

Moving carefully, I helped Mikayla stand. She shook from head to toe. "I don't feel so good," she said.

The aftereffects of using magic when you've been suppressing it for so long often imitates the flu. Plus, she'd just witnessed one hell of a scary scene. A scene she probably didn't understand, but she would, once I laid everything out for her about her abilities.

I took her hand and guided her toward the stairs. "You can lie down in my office. Come on."

We found Nikita, or rather she found us by sticking her cold nose into my left hand. My palm stung a bit, but overall, it seemed to have survived the brunt of the fire ball with little more than a blister or two. I wrapped it under Nikita's collar and we followed the glowing bowl.

Keisha joined us, and she and I hugged each other in relief. For no reason other than stress, we both started laughing, Mikayla and Nikita standing by quietly. Soon our laughter ran out of control and tears streamed from my eyes as I leaned on her.

Surviving supernatural dodgeball can do that to a person.

With Keisha's beautiful laughter echoing around me, I felt renewed.

I want to live, I told the dark night above and anyone up there who might be listening. *I definitely want to live.*

CHAPTER FOURTEEN

"Surprise!" My friend and WA cohort, Liddy, yelled as the three of us and Nikita entered my office. As expected, Gabriel had headed straight for the ice cream.

The office was totally decked out for a slumber party. A very girlie slumber party, but tasteful girlie. Apparently Barbie and Strawberry Shortcake had done the redecorating but in a classy, grown-up way, since everything from the furniture to the strings of fairy lights hanging from the ceiling was in various shades of pink, purple and chocolate brown.

Five hot pink sleeping bags lay on the floor, circling a spread of giant bowls filled with popcorn, chips and dips, pop on ice, and Dove chocolates in every flavor. Just seeing the colored candy wrappers, all jumbled together in a sparkly purple bowl, gave me a moment's joy. There were other candies too. Keisha's favorite, KitKats. Em's Snickers.

Piles of pillows, incredibly soft looking blankets, brand new silk pajama sets and a stack of fashion magazines littered the floor where my desk had been. A separate area had cushy zebra-striped chairs and a complete nail station with dozens of polishes in all shades.

Even after everything I'd been through, the sight made the girl in me very happy.

Emilia came in through the outside door with a pile of board games and a Ouija board in her hands, took one look at me, and set the games down. She licked a finger and rubbed what I guessed was soot and ash off my left cheek. "My god, Amy. What happened to you?" She sniffed the air around my hair. "What is that smell? Is it your...?"

"Singed hair." I shrugged, feeling a tad shaky now that the adrenaline was wearing off, but also pissed that my hair—which was unruly at best even on a good day—was now a lopsided mess. "The Pyro demon attacked again. She's gone for good this time, though."

Em took hold of my wrists, held my arms away from my body and looked me over. I didn't need her expression to tell me I looked like a walking disaster. She, on the other hand, was perfectly put together in a linen dress and white sandals. "Luc said you were safe here."

"I was on the roof, which apparently isn't safe, even with wards on it. The Pyro got through them somehow, but in here, we have heavenly protection because of Gabriel. Evil can't get through that."

At least I hoped it couldn't. I was damned tired of fighting for my life.

I plopped down on a pink velvet chaise lounge, sinking into the soft upholstery with a sigh. It was almost as comfortable as Keisha's pillow top mattress. I motioned at the sleeping bags and fairy lights twinkling above us. "You guys didn't have to do all this."

Liddy sat next to me, smiling like it was Christmas. "We *didn't* do this." She gave Em a questioning look and Em shook her head.

"We thought *you* decorated the office for the slumber party."

My brain was working at half capacity, but it didn't take a genius or even a fully functioning frontal lobe to figure out the culprit.

Luc. He'd done this.

For me.

"Damn it," I said, pinching the bridge of my nose.

Keisha examined the sleeping bags and picked the one she wanted...a pink leopard print. She kicked off her shoes and grabbed a handful of KitKats. She knew what I was thinking, because she was thinking the same thing. "'Damn it'? That's your response?" She shook her head and beaded braids flew in an arc. "I'd say, 'holy cow, the dude loves me', would be more accurate."

Em's brows shot up, lifting her bangs. "Lucifer did this?"

And then she said, "Lucifer did this," and it wasn't a question, but a statement tinged with awe. "We never got to have sleepovers growing up. You always felt cheated."

I say again, loves sucks. I ignored the approval in Em's eyes, walked over and grabbed the monster bowl of popcorn before settling back on the chaise. I kicked off my shoes and pulled my feet under me. "So let's get this party started. What do we do besides stuff our faces and do our nails?"

Nikita came over and laid her head on my lap. Mikayla stood in the corner, staring at the sleeping bags but her eyes were distant.

"I don't know," Liddy admitted next to me. "My sister and I never got invited to slumber parties and the one we tried to have in second grade...no one came to."

My heart cracked a little, hearing the hurt in her voice.

Keisha shrugged. "I never did the sleepover thing either."

We all looked at Mikayla. She blinked, mentally returning to the room, and nodded self-consciously. "Um, well, we gossip about other girls, talk about hot guys, do our nails and play games."

I so needed to talk to her. Didn't seem like we were going to have a chance to talk alone, though, unless I dragged her out to the ice cream parlor.

Or got everyone else to go out there. "The only thing missing is ice cream," I said. "Why don't we all go out to the shop and make the most wild, incredible concoction we can come up with?"

Ice cream, in my opinion, is a universal problem solver. No matter how bad the situation, it always makes things better.

Everyone's eyes brightened. Everyone's but Mikayla's,

Liddy jumped up from the chaise and led the way, Keisha and Em following. Mikayla stayed in the corner and I made a production of putting the bowl of popcorn back in the center of the sleeping bag circle. "That was intense up there, wasn't it?" I said, pointing a finger at the fairy-light bedecked ceiling.

Nikita watched both of us with her serious, intelligent gaze.

Mikayla jerked her head in a brief nod, but wouldn't meet my eyes.

"Mikayla, I'm sorry I couldn't introduce this idea to you in a nicer way, but I...I'm a..."

Her gaze snapped to my face, her chest heaving with pent up emotion. "You're a witch, aren't you?"

My obvious surprise must have shown on my face. She gave me a derisive shrug of her shoulders. "I read, okay? Paranormal stuff. And I watch *Supernatural* and *The Vampire Diaries*. I'm not a complete idiot."

Okay, so she'd been educated about witches and magic via pop culture. I could work with that. Hell, *The Vampire Diaries* had taught me a few things. "I'm a natural born witch, yes."

"And these other people—" she waved a hand toward the ice cream shop "—they're witches too. You're a coven."

"Not exactly." I fumbled around in my brain, trying to think of ways to explain the menagerie of Christian, Wiccan and occult representatives under my roof. "The important thing is that you're a witch as well, and your powers are trying to break free. Which makes you a prize to both the sides of good and evil. Your magic is special. Untainted. There are members of Heaven and Hell who would like to strip you of that magic. Use it for their own purposes."

Alarm crossed her face. I rushed to reassure her. "Don't worry. I'm going to help you. I've already been helping you, in fact. The priest who's stalking you? He's my guardian angel. I asked him to keep an eye on you since both Lucifer and Gabriel would like to get their hands on your powers."

Her brow furrowed. "*My* powers? I don't have any powers. I'm not a witch."

Denial was normal. One step at a time. "Your powers are in an embryonic stage. You're older than most witches when they come into their magic, but trust me, your powers are ready to bloom. They did in fact, upstairs on the roof. It was your magic that helped me send that fire ball back at the

71

pyromaniac." I took a step toward her and smiled. "You saved my life. Both our lives."

She shook her head, backing up against the wall. I noticed the charm necklace glowed softly where it lay on her breastbone.

"Your magic is nothing to be afraid of, Mikayla. You just have to learn how to control it and protect yourself." I eyed the necklace. "Where did you get that necklace?"

Her hand went to the charms and she rubbed them with her fingers. Their glow brightened, and I noticed Nikita moving closer to us as if she felt Mikayla's stress and wanted to offer comfort. "My grandmother gave it to me on my thirteenth birthday. It belonged to my mother. She died when I was ten."

The words and sigils inscribed on the charms were probably meant to dampen her magic, keep it under control. Maybe even protect her from someone. But why? "I'm sorry about your mother. How did she die?"

It was a personal question and I wasn't sure she would answer, but she did after a deep breath. Her voice was almost a whisper and tears brightened her eyes. "She was killed. Stabbed, on the steps of Immaculate Conception. Her murderer was never caught." She brushed tears off her cheeks with vengeance. "That's why I freaked out when the priest started following me. I thought maybe he was the…the…killer. I know that sounds terrible, accusing a priest of murder, but I felt something weird inside me every time he was around. Like my mother was telling me to get away from him."

Way to go, Ceph. No wonder she'd been completely freaked over his presence. He could have at least been stealthier about keeping an eye on her.

I was curious as to why Mikayla's mother had been killed, especially on the church's steps, and I bet it had to do with her being a witch. Maybe even Grandma was a witch, but after her daughter's death, decided the only way to protect Mikayla was to suppress her powers. "Do you ever take the necklace off?"

"Why? What does that matter?"

She wasn't going to like what I was going to say. "Your mother was a probably a witch and her murder might have been because of that. Your grandmother was trying to protect you from whatever killed your mother, so she charmed that necklace. After her death, though, the magic inside you couldn't be contained."

Mikayla blanched. "I've taken it off a couple times, but whenever I do, I feel sick. Like now. Except I'm wearing the necklace." The charms dropped from her fingers. "What happened on the roof? That…that woman…she was a witch too."

I started to say, *not exactly*, again, but thought better of it. The time for easing her into all this was well over. Her life was in danger, not just from Gabriel wanting to possess her body or Luc wanting to take her soul. "She was a demon assassin sent to kill me. You and Nikita unfortunately got caught in the crossfire."

For a few seconds, Mikayla said nothing, but from the look on her face, her brain was in overdrive. She was putting things together at rapid speed and her features hardened. "Why are they trying to kill you? Because of your powers? Do they want your magic or are they afraid of you becoming too powerful?"

Both were noble reasons to try and kill me. Unfortunately neither was true. "Actually, their boss doesn't like me. She's in love with Luc, my ex, who's still in love with me. It's…complicated."

"She's jealous, so she sends demons to *kill* you? Over a guy?" Mikayla frowned. "Is she a witch too?"

I shook my head. "She's the Queen of Hell."

She silently mouthed *queen of hell* while raising her eyebrows. Then she shook her head in tired disgust. "You'd think she'd have more important, like *supernaturally* important, things to worry about, being the Queen of Hell. Guess even she can go a little wacky when it comes to love, huh?"

Love and jealousy weren't only human emotions. Witches, demons, angels…we all got caught up in them.

I opened my mouth to answer her and was cut off by a voice behind me. "Amy?"

My heart leapt and I whirled around.

Adam, the first man God ever created, stood in the doorway of my office, looking for the world like a man who'd just been to Hell and back.

CHAPTER FIFTEEN

"Adam!" I flew across the room and grabbed hold of him without thinking and was rewarded by him making a painful face and flinching away. My blood turned cold. "Holy Hell. What did Lilith do to you?"

He rubbed a hand gently over his ribs and let me guide him to the chaise. "Just a few bruises."

His gazed bounced over the room, seeing the decked out slumber party setup instead of my office. Mikayla stepped forward. "Do you need a drink of water or something?"

I introduced the two of them and Adam declined the water. Mikayla grabbed Nikita by the collar and hustled her out the door, saying, "I'll just go talk to Keisha about the work schedule."

I didn't stop her from taking the dog into the ice cream shop. Once she was gone, I brushed a lock of brown hair out of Adam's eyes. "I'm so, so sorry about all of this. I know it doesn't look like it, but I was working on a plan to get you out of Hell. How did you escape?"

Again he grimaced but not from physical pain, it seemed. "Lucifer. He was there. He must have said something to Lilith and the next thing I knew, I was being escorted out of Hell. He gave me a message for you."

He swallowed hard and looked down at the floor, clenching his teeth.

I hated that he detested Luc so much. After what Lilith had done because of her jealousy, he might hate me now too. I swallowed the tightness in my throat. "What did Luc say?"

"He said to tell you, you're safe now." Adam's gaze met mine and I saw bitterness in his eyes. Behind that, I saw a flicker of something that didn't mesh up. It was there and gone in an instant, and yet I saw it for what it was. It was hard. It was cold.

It was evil.

So evil, in fact, my magic—dark as it was—drew back.

Adam, evil? No. That wasn't possible.

But when he spoke, there was a sinister edge to his words. "Your apartment burning, you being sick. Lilith did those things to you because of him. Because of Lucifer. And yet, you see him as some kind of hero, don't you? Because he came to my rescue?"

A memory of the horse-faced woman on the street the night my apartment burned rose in my mind. In some ways, Luc was a hero, but the way Adam said the word, it sounded ugly.

I squeezed one of his hands. "It's over now. You're back, Lilith's assassins are dead, and you and I are both safe. All we have to do is get you healed. Keisha's mighty handy in the healing department. She can have you fixed up in no time."

He shot up off the chaise, regardless of his injuries, and stared me down, eyes unforgiving. "It's not over. Eve's still down there. Still at Lilith's mercy. As soon as I figure how to free her, I'm going back. I only stopped by to tell you that you're safe. According to Luc, anyway."

Once more, the edge in his voice said he didn't trust Luc and neither should I. What bothered me more was his determination to save Eve. Of course he wanted to save her, but there was more to it than simply being a hero.

Standing up, I ignored the pain in my heart and the tone in his voice. I hoped the flicker of evil I'd seen behind his eyes was, in reality, the overhead fairy lights playing tricks on me. "I'll drive you home. We can stop at the clinic on the way and let a doctor look you over if you don't want Keisha to."

"Look, Amy…" he trailed off and again dropped his attention to the floor as if he couldn't meet my gaze straight on. Intuition sparked and I had the crazy idea he wanted to break up with me, then and there. I reached out and touched his arm, trying to get him to look me in the eye. Trying to show him I loved and cared about him. Maybe it was too little, too late, but I couldn't stand not touching him.

My touch did no good. He shifted away from my hand. "I'll call you tomorrow."

Sure he would. I took a step back, hurt crawling inside my chest. *He's been through hell, literally*, I reminded myself. *Give him some space.* "Sure."

It actually surprised me when he kissed my forehead. A chaste kiss. A disappointingly chaste kiss when all I wanted was to throw my arms around him and make him feel better. And myself too.

"Be safe," I said to his back as he went through the door. He continued on as if he hadn't heard.

Alone in the land of pink and pinker, I sank down on the chaise, rubbed my eyes and wondered if Adam and I would ever have a normal relationship, untainted by our pasts.

Mikayla, Nikita, Em, Liddy and Keisha returned. They insisted unanimously that we have the slumber party even though Lilith had been muzzled.

Kicking things off, I asked them what they thought about me and Adam being a normal couple.

Emilia, who was finishing the last of her ice cream and situating herself in the chair to allow Liddy to paint her nails, chuckled cynically. "Normal? Who has a normal relationship? No one I've ever known, that's for sure."

Keisha nodded from her sleeping bag, a Hollywood gossip magazine open in front of her. "Human or not, normal is a sitcom pipedream." She held the magazine up and waved it in front of me. "See these people? All miserable in love even though they're rich and famous."

"My friend Susan and her husband were plain ol' regular people who'd been married for twenty years," Liddy said, filing one of Em's fingernails. "Her high school sweetheart, Rob, came back from Southern California, a total washed up surfer dude, and Sue left her husband, a real stand up guy with a big 401K to run away with him."

Mikayla listened quietly on top of her sleeping bag, staring at the ceiling and stroking Nikita's head. I let go of a loud sigh and leaned my head against the back of the chaise. This was one time being magic-free and in the normal, human category felt good. I wasn't alone. Everyone had love troubles.

"Sometimes overcoming all the crap in your past is what makes the relationship stronger," Mikayla said out of the blue. "That's how you know you're meant to be together."

She sounded far too old and wise for her eighteen years. Maybe she read romance novels like Keisha, or had watched too many rom-com movies. Maybe, like me, she'd learned a few things from *The Vampire Diaries*.

Still, I liked her theory. A sense of renewed hope took root inside me. "Tomorrow, I'm going to make it up to Adam. We'll start over. I'll stay away from Luc, Adam will stay away from Eve after we rescue her from the pit, and we'll keep our pasts where they belong…in the past."

Keisha gave me the *what planet are you living on* look but I ignored her. It was my slumber party. If I wanted to be Polly Anna and think on the bright side, I had every right. Hope was alive in Amy Atwood's heart. Especially since it was the only thing I had left.

The idea of a slumber party isn't to actually slumber from what I've heard, but unlike a bunch of preteen girls, we already knew what boys wanted, how to French kiss and had solved most of the world's other problems before midnight. The only difficult part was convincing Mikayla to stay.

Luckily, curiosity got the better of her. She asked a question about our various witch proclivities and that's all it took. Em started in on a speech about Wicca and its tenets, but Keisha cut her off halfway through and said we should let Mikayla ask questions about what she was interested in. The rest of us agreed, so Mikayla asked and we answered—a magical version of Twenty Questions—giving her a fairly encompassing lesson on the various beliefs represented.

Eventually, the talk died down. The fairy lights dimmed. I was the last to give in and snuggle into my sleeping bag and it felt just as good as my old bed. The only things missing were Cain and Abel, but I knew they were safe and sound at Keisha's place.

Around me, my sister and friends lay sleeping, their deep, even breathing reassuring me. Witch or human, magically gifted or magic-free, experienced or innocent, we were together and we were strong in our love for each other and our varying beliefs. We could handle anything life threw at us as long as we stayed that way.

I fell asleep feeling at peace for the first time in days.

CHAPTER SIXTEEN

There's nothing like waking to a monster Rottweiler staring you in the face.

I woke from a deep sleep, heart racing, Nikita standing over me, her head hung low as if she'd been watching me snore.

She nudged my shoulder with her nose and backed away, seeming to want me to follow her. Probably needed to go outside. The clock on the wall read three a.m., and I mentally groaned, wanting nothing more than to snuggle back down and return to sleep. That was the nice thing about owning cats— they did their business inside and never woke you in the middle of the night for a pee break.

Everyone else was asleep. Rubbing my eyes and yawning, I climbed out of my comfy sleeping bag. The moment I stood, Nikita wagged her stumpy tail and made haste for the door connected to the alley. She pawed the door and made a whining noise. Grabbing her leash, I put a finger to my lips and shushed her, so she didn't wake the others. Which was probably pointless since she was a dog and didn't understand the gesture any more than I understood canine language.

I clipped the leash to her collar and unlocked the door slowly, the bolt making a soft *snick*. Nobody woke, so I eased the door open and out into the night we went.

The alley was lit by a single bulb above the door. The night air was warm and humid and my silk pajama bottoms stuck to my skin. I'm really more of a cotton gal for this very reason. Silk and satin look pretty but there's nothing better than lightweight cotton in summertime sleep apparel.

I headed down the dark alley toward the street. There was a grassy lot next to the park on the other side of the street that ran in front of my building, perfect I thought for a dog. As we passed the still overflowing dumpster, however, Nikita put the brakes on. She sniffed the dumpster, the ground, the building. I figured she was fascinated by all the garbage-y smells and tried to get her to keep moving, but she was stubborn and unmovable.

She didn't seem too interested in peeing either. I could have used my Hulk strength to drag her, but I didn't want to hurt her, just get her moving again. Sighing, I stared up at the night sky, watching clouds moving across the stars and waited for her to get the sniffing jones out of her system.

I thought about Adam and hoped he was sleeping soundly after his ordeal. I wondered what he was going to tell the guys at the station. What he was going to tell the detective looking into his disappearance. How he was going to get Eve out of the pit.

Closing my eyes and leaning against the cool, rough bricks of the building, my mind also wandered down the Luc trail. Where was he? Still in Hell with Lilith? What had he said to her to secure Adam's freedom? Why hadn't he come back and told me I was safe to my face? Was he avoiding me? Trying to stay on Lilith's good side? Had he made some kind of deal with her? Promised her he'd never see me again?

A breeze, hot and humid, caressed my bare skin and I shivered. What if Luc was truly gone from my life? Wasn't that what I'd wanted for months? To be free of him and his dark magic so I could live a happy life with Adam?

My heart did an unbalanced *thudthud* against my ribcage. I was grateful Luc had freed Adam from Lilith, but at what price? Way deep down inside, I was suddenly scared that I couldn't live without him.

Don't be silly. It's time to move on.

Nikita's cold nose nudged my hand, startling me. I looked down at her and found I wasn't looking down as far as normal. She seemed to have grown taller. Her head now came to my waist and her nose eagerly sniffed at my wrist like I'd rubbed bacon on it or something. Thinking the shadows were causing me to see weirdly, I blinked and pushed off the wall.

Nope, it wasn't the shadows and it wasn't my tired eyes either. Nikita was now nearly twice as big as she had been.

"What the…" I mumbled, taking another step back.

Raising her head, her gaze met mine and her eyes shone much too bright considering there was so little light in the alley. My stomach fell and my instincts screamed *run*.

But run where? And how could I outrun a dog? Especially one who was now probably as tall as Gabriel if she stood on her hind feet.

"You're not really a dog, are you?"

She cocked her head to one side and whatever glamour she'd been using to look like a beautiful Rottweiler fell completely away. She was still striking, broad and muscled, face still intelligent, but one of her ears had a notch out of it and a long scar ran down the front of her chest. Another smaller one cut across one eyebrow. The short, shiny Rottweiler coat now stood up in spikes all over her body, the hairs sticking straight out like needles.

In response to my question, she lifted the edges of her lips and showed me her canines. They, too, were bigger than I remembered, seeming to grow longer even as I watched. A low growl emanated from her chest and the hairs on the back of my neck shot to attention. My magic drew back, just like it had when I'd seen evil behind Adam's eyes.

This was dark magic. Really dark. As dark as Luc's and then some.

Skirting Nikita, trying to get back to the door, I lowered my voice and spoke in what I hoped was comforting tones. Whether for her or me, I wasn't sure. "Easy there, Nikita. I don't know what's going on, but I'm your friend, remember?"

She jumped sideways in a fluid Spiderman-type move, blocking my path to the door. Her muzzle trembled as she growled again low in her throat. I jumped back, bare shoulders ramming into the rough brick of the neighboring building, and stuck my hands out in an attempt to fend her off. As if that would do much good. "No, no. Bad dog."

Lame, I know, but really, I had no other thought than, *bad dog*.

She sprung. It happened so fast I didn't even see her move. One second she was still a good two feet away and the next, she had her jaws clamped down on my left wrist and I was falling to the ground, her on top of me.

I cried out and tried to roll away, but went nowhere, her weight pinning me to the gross alley ground, her teeth, both upper and lower incisors, cutting through skin and muscles, and clamping my forearm between them with bone crushing force.

White hot pain shot up my arm and into my chest. My heart, pumping fast, pounded against my ribcage with a fierce fight-or-flight urgency. Alongside it, my magic reared and pulsed with a reflexive counterattack like a second heartbeat. There was no fleeing in this case and all my instincts screamed for me to use whatever tool was at my disposal to fight. Yet when I opened my mouth to utter a defensive spell—throwing my oath out the window, and not really giving a damn—nothing came out. My vocal chords were frozen.

Blood ran in dark streams down my arm, dripping onto my chest. Balling my free hand into a fist, I hit Nikita on her now elongated snout as hard as I could, hoping my superhuman strength would smash it. She didn't even flinch, and in her eyes, now the size of golf balls to match the rest of her, I saw the fires of Hell.

Hell hound. She was a freakin Hell hound.

Bad bad dog!

I'd never seen a real, live Hell hound before. I'd seen various renditions of them in movies and a few of Cephiel's books in his Father Leonard office at Immaculate Conception. The real thing, by far, was scarier.

Especially when its enormous paws were on your chest and it was draining you of blood.

A wave of dizziness made everything, including her face and my blood-soaked arm, swim in front of my eyes. A loud buzzing sound took up residence in my ears, and my pulse, which had been pounding hot and thick in my neck, slowed. I tried to cry out again, tried calling to everyone in my mind, including Luc, but my thoughts turned fuzzy and dreamlike, everything shimmering.

My heart skipped a beat and then another. Black dots danced in front of my eyes. I blinked and a tear escaped the corner of my eye. Pain radiated through my entire chest and spread down my spine. Even if Nikita hadn't been on top of me, I wouldn't have been able to move. I was paralyzed.

As warm blood seeped over my chest and pooled under me, I knew I was dying. My heartbeat and pulse continued to slow and the harder I fought it, the less progress I made, until a deep heaviness that had nothing to do with Nikita's weight consumed me.

A strange tugging started inside me, as if an organ was trying to tear away from my body. At first I thought it was my heart fighting the growing lethargy in order to keep beating. Then I realized it was something else entirely.

My soul.

It was trying to escape.

Paralyzed inside and out, I still tried to fight, but it was no use. My eyelids grew heavy and kept fluttering shut. Over and over again, I jerked them open, like I was fighting sleep.

I *was* fighting sleep. Eternal sleep.

As my vision dimmed and everything shrank to a pinpoint at the end of a dark tunnel, I sent one more mental call out to the Universe. Maybe it was my imagination, but I thought I heard Mikayla shout my name from far, far way.

I also heard her shout, "Bad dog!" and a small part of me gave a mental laugh. I was delirious, obviously, but I latched onto the sound of her voice as she threw insults at Nikita and called to the others for help. Instinctively I reached for her and her untainted magic in my mind.

Right before I shut my eyes for the final time, before my breathing stopped and my heart gave one last beat, I saw her face instead of Nikita's staring down at me.

CHAPTER SEVENTEEN

There was nothing…no pain, no light, no thoughts.

And then there was.

Brilliant light flashed under my eyelids.

A falling sensation.

The smell of smoke and burning flesh.

Blistering heat slithering over my skin.

In the distance, a familiar crackling and popping noise.

The same tugging sensation I had just experienced engulfed me again, except in a reverse way. My soul wasn't leaving my body—it was entering it.

Hard.

Wham! I did a face plant on a hot stone floor, the force of impact jarring every bone in my body. Then came my soul a split-second later, slamming into me like a speeding freight train.

Brain cells cocked and fired.

This is what a bug feels like when it hits the windshield of a semi doing ninety on the interstate.

I didn't even try to move. I wasn't sure I *could* move. For long minutes, I simply lay still, smelling the tainted smoke, listening to the crackling of fires, feeling the stifling, slippery heat coating my skin. Forget the bug getting hit by a semi. With this heat, I felt like a Barbie in the melting house of Amy fire.

My heart did a weird *thud* in my chest, like someone hit me there with a fist. Several uncomfortable seconds passed as it tried and failed to find its old rhythm. Something clicked finally, and it found a new one that seemed to work. More brain cells woke up.

If my heart was beating, I wasn't dead, right?

I could breathe and wiggle my fingers and toes. Cracking an eye open, I scanned the area I could see without lifting my head. My cheek was definitely lying on a stone floor, humidity covering it with a sheen of moisture. I sensed, more than heard, things slithering around me. The sound reminded me of the whisper of tissue paper made when Destructo Boy Duncan was throwing it out of gift bags during his birthday party.

Snakes was my first thought, although I wasn't sure why. Lying on the floor, I saw none, and yet I definitely sensed a snake-like presence moving and undulating around me.

Although there was fire and smoke, the place was dim and shadowed. Skeletal tree roots, covered with black moss, popped out of the ground on one side. Vines dripped from the branches.

Movement to the left caught my eye and I shifted enough to follow it, pain racing down the back of my head and into my neck. The sound of slithering met my ears again, and I realized the vines were moving. Gliding and rippling in the trees.

Apparently, I'd landed in a Tim Burton film. Lucky me. Pretty sure there was no white rabbit in a waistcoat coming to my rescue, though.

Gritting my teeth, I pushed up on my elbows, blew a heavy sigh to lift the hair out of my face, and noticed my left wrist was fine. The only signs Nikita had used me as a chew toy were four straw-sized puncture wounds, two on each side. The skin around them puckered, but the blood was gone. Gingerly, I touched the puckered spots and a deep ache resulted, but overall, there wasn't much pain and obviously, not much to show for her draining the life out of me. Damn dog.

Through the smoke, my gaze followed a path of carpet the color of blood across the stones to steps and a raised dais. An enormous throne was perched on the stage area and someone was sitting in it, but the details were fuzzy because of the smoke. I could see her boots, though. The black and gold platform leather boots had heels so spikey and tall, the owner either had an extreme shoe fetish or never actually intended to walk in them.

Anyone with shoes like that had my attention. Add to the fact the owner of the fetish boots was sitting on what appeared to be a matching gold and black throne made from—I squinted my eyes to see through the smoke—skulls, and I was more than curious. I was fascinated.

And more than a little grossed out.

Rising to hands and knees, I glanced around, hoping this was some sort of crazy shoe heaven—instead of what the nagging voice in my head suggested it was—and there were endless racks of outlandish boots, stiletto heels and pimped out wedges. So much so, I could spend eternity wearing a different pair of outlandish footwear, every hour and never run out.

I would be the Imelda Marcos of Heaven.

That thought alone cheered me considerably, until the smoke cleared for a moment and my gaze landed on a pile of skulls next to the throne, gleaming white and built up into a table, upon which a whip slithered and coiled like a snake.

Oh, gross. It *was* a snake, not just one, but dozens of the slippery things, and that didn't fit with my idea of a Heaven in which Imelda was in charge.

My knowledge of snakes was limited, but the ones on the table looked like asps if the Indiana Jones movies were an accurate resource. They twisted and curled around each other like the vines in the trees. Their tongues darted out and back in, beady eyes watching me with an eagerness that made goose flesh rise all over my damp skin.

Shifting back to the fetish boots, I tilted my face to get a better view through the haze. Their owner wore a black crushed velvet dress that draped over a pencil-thin body like a second skin. A high slit in the skirt revealed a lot of thigh and red silk ribbons laced up the deep plunging V-neckline, but still showed off a good deal of her extremely pale cleavage. Straight black hair fell around her shoulders.

Dark magic poured off her.

Just not dark magic. Evil, dark magic. She was marinating in it.

Lilith.

Like the asps on the table, her eyes gleamed with a strange fervor. I could see them now through the smoke and haze. The translucent skin of her face was flawless except for blue tattoos encircling her temples. Similar tattoos laced her neck and thighs.

She was stunning, although not in a good way. Being in Hell for a couple of eons had taken its toll on her skin and those tattoos were just, well, icky. Maybe my eyes were malfunctioning, but I swear the tats pulsed, moving in rhythm with the snakes and the creeping tree vines.

For half a second, I wondered if I would burst into tears or hysterical laughter. Me. In Hell. Facing Lilith.

Enormous braziers burned with red flames behind her throne. Chandeliers the size of Gabe's wings hung in various places from a ceiling that resembled the night sky. A starless night sky, devoid of any moon, much like the one I'd just left behind on Earth. Who knew Hell had a view of space?

The walls resembled red curtains, pulsing and rippling as if blood was running down them in a constant waterfall. Everything else was covered in gilt, reflecting the lights and fires back at me through the haze.

A low thrumming sound vibrated over my skin. As I watched the rippling curtains, I realized the slow repetitive beat in my ears wasn't the sound of my heart. I placed a hand over my chest, expecting to feel a beat, but there was nothing. The sound echoing in my ear was the pulse, the heartbeat, of Hell.

For some reason, that freaked me out as much as being dead. Really dead. No heartbeat, no life.

I stood on wobbly legs. Why the hell—no pun intended—*was* I dead? Luc had said I was safe. He'd worked some kind of deal with Lilith, right? To free Adam and get me off her Most Wanted list?

But I was definitely dead and in the pit.

Bottom line, there are some things you'd rather not know so completely. There are some things that take so much strength to examine, it feels like a ten-ton elephant on your head. The realization Luc loved me had felt like that, but it'd also felt like eating the best chocolate in the world at the same time.

This knowledge, about being in Hell, sucked. The problem with knowledge like this was, once you knew it, you could never go back to denial. Not really. Your brain could reject an idea and your heart could shore itself up with defiance and dissent, but your cells knew. Your blood knew.

A sharp sadness came over me. I was dead. Stinking dead and in Hell. Sweat collected in my elbows, the back of my knees. I shook with the truth, anger filling me like cement, making me hard and unmovable.

Anger is my go-to emotion. When bad stuff happens, I get angry. When I'm scared, I mold it into anger. Anger is a lot easier for me to deal with. Easier for me to channel than other emotions.

But anger makes it hard to think, and I needed to think. Someone, namely the skank in front of me who was still watching me with curious fascination, wasn't playing by the rules. I'd have bet my last pair of Louboutins—if they hadn't gone up in the fire—that Lilith had lied to Luc about leaving me alone. She'd made sure he and Adam thought I was safe and then she'd had her *dog* take me down.

The dark magic below my feet rose from the ground, drawn to me like a magnet to steel. I could feel it enter the soles of my feet, anchoring me there, and it felt solid and welcome. Not the air magic I was accustomed to, but earth magic. It surged up my legs and into my stomach. When it hit my heart and the spot my magic should have been, it flashed through the rest of me like lightning, snapping my head back and electrifying me from head to toe.

And that's when I decided. If Lilith didn't have to play by the rules, neither did I.

The Vampire Diaries had taught me a lot, but there was one thing I'd learned from Angel, the hottest and smartest vamp on TV. No one was unstoppable.

Now if I only had a strategic playbook to refer to. Something straightforward like…How To Take Lilith Down In Three Easy Steps. Even a simple plan would have been nice, but as I stood there trying to think of some way to face Lilith and come out of the situation alive, my mind was blank. Not blank actually, but filled with that lovely white hot anger.

That's the thing with anger. You can pretend it's not there, but it still fills every crevice, every crease.

I didn't just want to live again. I wanted revenge.

I sent an S-O-S to everyone in Heaven, Hell and on Earth I could think of. Cephiel, my so-called guardian angel—fat lot of good he was doing me. Lucifer, who was supposed to be keeping an eye on things and, *hello*, didn't he realize I was in his territory? Would've been nice if he'd shown up. Didn't all newly dead souls have to check in or something?

And finally, I swallowed my pride and sent a demanding request to Gabriel. If he could send Adam back to Earth, he could yank me out of Hell. It was probably too much work for Angelzilla, he was so lazy and ungrateful, so I added that if I stayed in Hell, he could kiss his ice cream supply buh-bye.

On the opposite side of the asp table, a woman sat on the stage next to Lilith's throne, naked, with an enormous collar of spikes clamped around her neck. Her head was tilted down, gaze on the floor, hair curtaining her face. She must have felt my stare because she raised her eyes slightly to meet mine.

Ah ha. I walked up the carpeted aisle to get closer. "Eve?"

My voice was back! Triumph flooded me at the sound. I was hoarse, but still, I could talk again. "Adam and Luc told me you were here. What happened?"

Her answer was a glance at Lilith who still watched me with her snake-like stare roving over every part of my body with calculating intensity.

Glancing down, I was relieved I didn't look too bad. This obviously wasn't shoe heaven and I was definitely dead, but at least I wasn't doing an impression of a character from Zombieland. Seemed like a plus. When Lilith's gaze hit my stomach, I automatically sucked it in.

So sue me for having a little pride. When your ex's ex is sizing you up, you don't want your stomach sticking out.

Stealing another look around in case there were any doors with large Exit signs above them, I saw dozens of hunched over women moving listlessly in the shadows. Some carried platters of food and drink, others fanned the braziers. All of them had spiked collars around their necks and chains between their ankles and wrists. Most of them were naked with open wounds, blisters and bruises covering their bodies. Some had shaved heads, others had long, stringy hair.

Up to that point, I didn't think I could hate Lilith any more than I already did.

Surprise. I could.

There were various animals moving in the shadows as well. Night creatures and salivating wolves. More snakes twining around massive columns, up the undulating walls of blood and over more skulls and bones scattered in the corners. Beetles and moths scurried and fluttered everywhere.

Nikita, however, was nowhere in sight.

Good thing, 'cuz if I saw her again, I was gonna…

What, Amy? Kill her? She's a Hell hound, for pity's sake.

Okay, maybe I couldn't kill her, but if I ever saw her again, I was going to tweak her stubby tail until she squealed like a pig.

Lilith raised one hand and snapped her fingers. Her fingernails belonged on a cougar, and not the over-forty human female variety either. Long, red, and filed to wicked looking points, they clicked as she drummed them against the jewel encrusted arm of her gilded skull chair.

From the shadows, a tall, muscular female stepped forward in response. Her skin was the color of caramel, her tightly cropped hair, black and shiny as oil. She was dressed from head to toe in black and her eyes met mine with equal parts ruthlessness and intelligence. I knew immediately I wouldn't be tweaking her tail any time soon.

"Yes, your majesty," Nikita said to Lilith, her voice edged with a slight British accent.

I narrowed my eyes at her. "You." I tried to think of something caustic to add, came up dry.

Lilith's mouth didn't move but her voice boomed clear as day, echoing off the walls and making the slaves jump. I admit, I jumped a little too. "You brought the wrong woman."

Nikita stood her ground, head held high. "I assure you, my queen, this is Amy Atwood."

"This?" Lilith made a disgusted face, tattoos lengthening as she frowned. "She looks so *ordinary*. Lucifer would never fall for such a pathetic version of me."

Version of *her*? Pathetic?

Was she joking?

She didn't look like the type to joke. Surreptitiously, I glanced down at myself again. While I wasn't a perfect size two or runway gorgeous, I wasn't exactly ugly. Maybe a little ordinary, I'd give her that, but still, someone needed a reality check if she thought she was the standard for beauty.

"I hate to break it to you, Lil, but you're not exactly a catch these days. If anything, Luc was probably looking for your opposite in every way."

The fires in the braziers flared and her fingernails froze in midtap. A muscle twitched under her left eye. Her energy, the blackest black magic I'd ever felt, slammed into me, knocking me backwards. "You dare speak to me?"

Righting myself, I gave her my best Keisha hairy eyeball impression. "You're the one who had me killed and brought here. What did you think would happen? I'd lie on the floor and quiver with fear? Of course I dare speak to you."

I took a step forward. As always my runaway mouth gave me a false sense of bravery. "I'm going to dare a lot more, too, so you might want to prepare yourself. You may have picked this fight, but I'm not a bug you can squash under those ridiculous stilettos. I plan to fight and fight dirty."

What was I saying? I couldn't take Lilith in a fight. Her power was as old as the Earth. As old as God's. Heck, she didn't even have to open her mouth to talk.

What was up with that anyway? Could she *be* more of a freak?

Nikita and Eve stared at me with humongous eyes and slack jaws. Apparently nobody talked to the queen bee like that.

What*ever.*

I expected Lilith to come out of her seat. To yell at me or flick one of her monster claws and fling me like a wet noodle against a wall. Maybe even set her wolves on me, or her snakes.

Instead, she sat back and laughed, lips curving and mouth opening. It was an eerie laugh that made me think of horror movies. The sound, and the way it rattled my composure, weirded me out. Big time.

"You have no magic here, witch."

Her tone was assured, self-righteous, and it pissed me off. My hand automatically touched the place over my heart and cold fear settled in the pit of my stomach. She was right. My magic didn't stir. It didn't react. I mentally called to it and got no response.

Because it wasn't there.

I don't know what I would have done if my powers had responded, but magic had always been a part of me. Even before the Barbie playhouse incident, it had hibernated inside me like a secret buried next to my heart. Now it was gone, baby, gone.

I was well and truly on my own. No magic. No power. The dark magic coming up from the ground wasn't mine. It was hers. And so far, there was no Heavenly intervention. Not even my ex, who was handy in the fire and brimstone department.

There was just me.

One hundred percent human, and apparently an ordinary one at that.

Not even that could stop my mouth, though. "So what exactly are you?" I leaned forward and eyed her tattoos. "Witch? Demon? Fallen angel? I don't really get why you're Queen of Hell instead of, say, Eve there. I mean, she's the gal who ate from the apple and brought sin into the world. Why doesn't she get to be queen?"

Eve sucked in a sharp breath. Lilith smirked, but the tattoos around her temples seemed to brighten. "Lucifer didn't tell you?"

The way she sort of purred his name gave me an idea of how to turn things around on her. While I'd thought I'd simply explain that Luc and I were no longer a couple and never would be again—although I had a few doubts about the veracity of that statement—I now saw that was the wrong angle to take.

Lilith loved Luc and wanted him for herself. My best card was to make her believe she would never have him, no matter what she did to me. "Luc and I...we don't *talk* much, if you get my meaning." I gave her an exaggerated wink and snickered under my breath.

Bingo. The blue tattoos turned dark and murky, her temples pulsing hard enough I saw the rise and fall of each beat. "I am not a lesser being such as you. I am God's counterpart. His equal."

Whoa. Her ego was as big as her throne. "So why aren't you in Heaven?"

Crossing one skinny leg over the other, she warmed to telling her side of the story. "God and I…had a falling out. He gave me this realm to rule over."

"I thought you were Adam's first wife, and you know, you defied God, he kicked you out of Eden and…"

Eve was shaking her head at me with little furtive movements back and forth. I had no idea what she was warning me about. I finished repeating the story Kitanna had told me and Cephiel had confirmed about Lilith, Adam and Luc. I did leave out the part about Gabriel. I didn't think it had much relevance and something told me to hold off on playing that card.

Lilith threw her head back and laughed again as if I'd said the punch line to a particularly hilarious joke. The tattoos on her neck quivered.

"What a ridiculous story," she said when she was done laughing at me. "Haven't you ever wondered why God doesn't have a companion? Why, if He is the Almighty and a single male entity of omnipotent power, He creates a female counterpart for Adam and not himself? Why He didn't simply create man and man alone, since that would truly be *in His own image?*"

Actually, I'd never given it any thought, but it made sense. God created Adam and then gave him a female companion, and yet God didn't have one? Sure, some people purported God was both male and female, so why hadn't he created humans to be both in one body as well?

Lilith saw me struggling to come up with a logical answer. Her lips quirked at my inability to do so. "I was God's companion. He insisted I come to Earth to view His silly little creation." She sniffed as if she found the whole thing ludicrous. "When I refused to take any interest, He decided to create man. A new pet. Someone who would appreciate Him and his work."

This time she shook her head, staring off in the distance. "All those angels, singing His praises and fawning over Him, and he couldn't stand the fact I was not impressed by His insignificant hobby."

The way she said, *hobby*, it sounded like a disease. "And so he, what? Kicked you out of Heaven because you weren't impressed with Earth?"

Her face softened slightly and a ghost of the beautiful woman she had once been surfaced for a split second. I mean it, she glowed. "When I saw Adam, I had a change of heart. He was perfect. Exquisite. As beautiful as any of Heaven's angels…"

She trailed off and a shiver of comprehension went down my spine. "You fell in love with Adam."

Her eyes flicked to me. "God became jealous."

And handed her divorce papers. "He kicked you out of Heaven for messing around with Adam."

The smirk returned and she petted Eve's head, long nails dragging through Eve's hair. I swear, I felt them scratching my own scalp, the way Eve flinched. "I was also banned from the Garden, and God then created Eve, but I wasn't done with Adam." She chuckled low in her throat. "I wasn't done with God."

The asps had become more frenzied in their writhing as she spoke, and when she drew out and emphasized *I wasn't done with God*, they hissed and bit each other, coiling up higher and higher into tall spirals before falling back onto the table. Lilith's tattoos were almost black and her eyes had that eager, hungry look to them again. Either she was delusional or she was telling the truth.

Delusional was the more appealing option, but my morally weak, ordinary human intuition told me it was also the wrong one.

Up to that point, I'd had the foolish hope, slim as it was, that I'd somehow trick her, out manipulate her. I had hoped to convince her to let me go, and by some miracle, I'd return to living on Earth.

Now, every last bit of that slim, wonderful hope died.

I was in Hell to stay.

The realization made me stagger, knees going weak and eyes blurring. Then whatever moral fiber I have that keeps me going no matter the odds, kicked in.

I blinked the tears away, straightened my spine and locked my knees. "*You* tempted Eve with the apple, didn't you? It wasn't Luc pretending to be a snake. It was you."

Her eyes widened fractionally and a pleased look passed over her face. The vines on her temples brightened once more. "God was so embarrassed I'd bested him at His own game, He covered up my involvement and placed the blame on Lucifer."

Eve bowed her head again.

Acid rose in my throat. "Luc took the fall for you in the history books, and why not? He'd already been cast out of Heaven for being a traitor. What was one more crime on his rap sheet?"

Lilith smiled as if I was a particularly good student, but her tattoos darkened. "But God banned me not just from Eden, but also from Earth. It was His creation, so He controlled its access. The only place left for me was Hell."

Anger at the injustice to Luc, to Adam, even to Eve, burned inside me as hot as the flames in the braziers. I crossed my arms and swallowed hard, forcing the acid back down. "That's nice and all, but what I want to know is, where are you going to go now?"

"Where am I going to go?" she mimicked. Her fingernails tapped the chair.

"You've been kicked out of Heaven and banned from Earth..." I gave her my best smirk and took a deep breath to shore up what little bravado I had left before I made my Hail Mary play. "And Hell, Lilith, isn't big enough for both of us."

CHAPTER EIGHTEEN

When my challenge registered with Lilith, everything went crazy. The fires flared toward the ceiling, forcing the women fanning them to jump back. The asps became so frenzied, they fell off the skull table in big splats of cold-blooded reptilian masses, scaly skins sizzling on the stone floor. The tattoos covering Lilith's body went pitch black, throbbing as though they would explode.

That's when I realized they weren't tattoos. They were veins.

I nearly lost my sleepover dinner of popcorn and chocolate, but this was no time for weakness of any sort. The meek might inherit the Earth, but the bold were going to conquer Hell. Me being the bold one in that equation.

Time to clarify my demands. "I want you out, Lil, and I want you out now."

The snakes stopped writhing. The slaves in the shadows froze in their tracks. Eve stiffened even more.

Lilith didn't move a single muscle for seconds, then her voice boomed throughout the room. Probably throughout all nine levels of Hell. "*You* want *me* out? You insignificant, powerless witch. How dare you threaten me!"

It took all my willpower not to cringe. So far, though, I hadn't seen any real evidence of her powers, other than her ability to speak without moving her lips. Sure, I'd been impressed the first time she'd done it, but now it seemed like a cheap parlor trick. She hadn't even stood from her chair, much less shapeshifted, thrown fireballs or poisoned a knife by wiping nail polish on it. Seemed to me, a god like herself would be showing off a little more.

"You're the one who had me killed and brought here." I gave Nikita a damning sneer. "I was perfectly happy on Earth, but now that I'm here, I plan to make myself at home."

I started climbing the steps to her throne, avoiding the asps as I went. Nikita grabbed my arm and tried to haul me off the stairs, but I kicked an asp her way and she shrieked and jumped back. Apparently Hell hounds didn't like snakes. Curious, but good to know.

I turned to Lilith and took the next step. The closer I got, the more I could see how fragile she looked, how skeletal and weak she appeared to be. I could work with that. "Besides, Luc's in love with me. Who do you think he and his demon army will back if I stage a coup?"

I didn't even know if Luc had a demon army, but something changed in her eyes. Since my magic was gone, I probably no longer had my superhuman strength either. Looking at Lilith with her translucent skin and emaciated body, I wasn't sure I needed it if we ended up in a physical brawl. Unless she speared me with one of her six-inch stilettos or filleted me with her nails, I could take her.

Of course, she was a god, or so she claimed. Somehow I thought Hell had zapped more than her beauty over the years. I hoped it had drained her omnipotence as well. Maybe the mother of demons was running on her reputation more than her actual power.

I threw my arms wide and surveyed my new kingdom, being careful not to turn my back on her. I gave Eve a sly wink, hoping she might provide back up when the time came. "All this is mine now." I faced Lilith again. "I can't thank you enough for bringing me here. Finally."

I did another twirl with my arms out like I was in the *Sound of Music* and ready to belt out a cheery tune. "I've been dreaming of this moment, the moment I became Queen of Hell, for seven long years."

She kicked out her top leg, nailing me with her stiletto in the soft flesh of my thigh hard enough to rip my satin pjs, draw blood and nearly topple me. I ignored the pain, smiling as she confirmed what I thought. If she were truly all-powerful, she wouldn't need to move a muscle to hurt me.

With one hand on my bleeding thigh, I leaned over and put my face close to hers. "You know, Gabriel told me all about you. Your strengths. Your weaknesses. He told me how to bring you down. Luc and I have it all figured out. How we're going to destroy you."

At that moment, Nikita overcame her fear of snakes and bolted up the wide stairs, but not before I saw my lies register with Lilith. The Hell hound grabbed for me and I ducked, sending her off-balance. She still managed to get hold of my wrist and yanked on it—the wrist she'd punctured and drained of blood—before both of us toppled onto Lilith and her throne.

With our combined weights, the sizable throne tipped on its back legs and wobbled there for a second. My face was buried in the high gold back, my breasts pressed into Lilith's face. One of Nikita's elbows was jammed in my back, her legs tangled in mine and both of us on top of Lilith.

I thought the chair would right itself, and I was almost disappointed, because toppling the skank seemed like good fun. And then Eve, who was still chained to the arm, jumped up and gave a big yank, and we all went over the backside of the platform.

A cat fight ensued and I was stabbed, scratched and kicked, but I wasn't completely sure who was doing what, and I gave as good as I got. Really, if I made it back to Earth, I was signing up for the WWF.

My head was slammed into the throne more than once and soon I had blood running into my eyes from a cut on my forehead. Someone's elbow caught me in the mouth and busted my lip open and more blood flowed. It got in my mouth and tasted like metal, causing my stomach to heave. At one point, Lilith threw me against the skull table, which was surprisingly sturdy, and pain like I'd never felt before burst in my ribcage. I could hardly breathe for several minutes, probably because I'd cracked a rib.

She wasn't as weak as I'd thought.

The slaves and animals had scattered into the fringes of the room the moment we sent the throne ass over tea kettle, and during the fight, we managed to knock over, not one, but a dozen of the braziers, sending fire and hot coals in all directions.

I managed to unhook Eve from the throne, but Lilith kneed me in the ribs and got hold of the chain still attached to Eve's neck collar. She was jerking Eve's chain, literally, while my hand was buried in Lilith's hair and someone, Nikita I presumed, was biting my calf.

Strong hands grabbed me from behind by the waist and yanked me backwards and against a sturdy warm body. A man, I was sure, who was tall and broad and emanating some righteous energy. I cried out, half in pain and half in wild girl-fighting abandon, as he lifted me off the ground, off Lilith.

Take that, I thought as I drove my elbow backwards, trying to hit him in the stomach. At the same time, I kicked back with my heels, hoping to make contact with a shin or two. Both moves failed as he sucked in his stomach, avoiding my elbow, and lifted me away from his torso so my feet swung free like I was running in space.

Panic pierced my fight-induced self-confidence. Lilith must have called in reinforcements and this guy was going to do what she couldn't…destroy me.

I raised my leg to give one last backward kick aimed at what I hoped were his balls when he said, "Don't even think about it, witch," and I froze in a cartoon-like pose.

"What in Hades is going on here?" Luc's voice roared over the ruckus.

Eve, Nikita and Lilith all froze, like me. I twisted my head to see him as he held me at arm's length, Gabriel at his side. Neither looked too happy to see me, but I have to say, seeing both of them, even Angelzilla with his usual annoyed scowl, made my heart do a happy dance.

Lilith dropped Eve's chain and Nikita helped the supposed queen to her feet. Luc set me down, put his hands on his waist and shook his head as he took in my bloody face and the mess we'd made of the throne. Then he squinted at me. "Your eyes," he murmured.

Before I could ask him what was wrong with them, Lilith made a fatal mistake. Okay, not *fatal*, since she was already dead, but you know what I mean. She made an enormous mistake. A real whopper.

She stepped toward me and grabbed me by the neck with the crushing strength of a pro-wrestler on steroids, lifting my entire body off the floor as she rose to her full height on those gargantuan heels. She wasn't as weak as

I'd suspected, but I'd noticed during our all-star wrestling extravaganza that most of her power seemed to be of the psychic kind, rather than the physical.

Holding me out toward Luc so he could get a good look at my bulging eyes and wagging tongue, not to mention my blood soaked face, she shook me at him as if I were nothing but a ragdoll. Her enraged psychic energy raised all the hair on my back of my neck. In my mind's eye, I saw her veins pulsing with it. "This is what you left me for? *This*?"

Let me just say, Luc's rage was equally exacting and beautiful to behold. When he's merely angry, his brow furrows a tiny fraction, his lips turn down and his eyes flatten, but his body language on the whole is controlled with steely restraint.

As he looked at Lilith, shaking a bleeding and battered me in front of him, his eyes were anything but detached. In fact, I'd never seen him so furious. It wasn't just his eyes that blazed with anger. His whole body fumed, and not with the piddlely human variety of fury either. He seethed wrath as if he were wrath itself. He seethed anger like…well, like a god.

"Put. Her. Down."

His voice, his words, echoed through the entire place, shaking the walls and cracking the floor under Lilith's feet. The slaves and assorted animals still hanging around, cowered and backed farther into the shadows.

I had both hands on Lilith's, trying to break her hold, but to no avail. I couldn't even break one of her ugly fingernails. My legs swung back and forth as I struggled in her grasp, my ribcage on fire and blood from all my wounds pooling under me.

I might have been dead, but I could still feel pain, and let me tell you, I was in pain.

I stopped fighting and went limp, my body exhausted. Inside my chest, my soul bumped against my heart and the spot where my magic had been, as if it was looking for a way out.

Lilith smirked. "Her soul is mine."

Ah, shit. Not my soul. I'd rather hand it over to Gabriel again than let Lilith have it.

"No." Luc's voice was as grim as his expression. "Her soul belongs to me."

It wasn't like I could disagree. My throat, including my vocal cords, was crushed under her hand. I did, however, notice a stirring in my extremities when Luc met my gaze. A stirring that raced up my limbs and tingled nerve endings all the way up to my scalp.

Gabe rippled his wings and said to Luc, "Can we wrap this up? I need to get back before sunrise."

A newfound strength coursed through me. I wiggled my fingers and then my toes. Maybe I was like a vampire now. You could hurt me, but you couldn't kill me unless you staked my heart.

Coool.

I glanced down at my thigh. It was no longer bleeding. In fact, the wound seemed to be healing on its own. I glanced to my left and saw Eve giving me a meaningful look, also trying to tell me something with her eyes. She'd look at me and then at Lilith's temples, neck, arms and legs.

The tattoos, er, veins.

Of course. Her power source. An image of the snakes turning on each other when I'd pissed her off surfaced. I needed to turn her power against her, but how?

When I was alive and I had one of these critical moments, I reached for a Dove or a scoop of Luscious Lime ice cream, to which I add a handful of gummie worms. Swear to God, works every time to jumpstart the creative side of my brain. Obviously, in my current state, that wasn't an option.

"I will never let you leave me," Lilith shouted at Luc without moving her lips. Seriously lame. She shook me again, hard enough my teeth rattled. "I will destroy this…this…*thing* before I let her take over Hell."

Luc frowned, perplexed it seemed at trying to figure out how I would take over, but Gabe had heard enough. He wasn't much into drama, unless he was watching *Days of Our Lives* or *The Real Housewives of New Jersey* with Keisha. He flicked one hand and my body fell out of Lilith's grip. I fell to the floor in a heap at Eve's feet. An asp slithered by, meeting my gaze with one liquidy eye.

"This…this…worthless human," Lilith seethed, giving Gabriel a look that said she would kill him if she could, "thinks she can take my place at your side!"

Luc let go of an exaggerated sigh. "You never were at my side, Lilith. We could never be partners. Equals. You have this level of Hell, I have the rest for that reason."

"Because I'm a god and you're nothing but a fallen angel."

He shook his head. "Because you've never loved anyone but yourself."

The two of them continued their standoff, Gabe tapped one foot and looked around as if bored. Eve bent down to examine my neck and help me sit up. I shifted my head, pretending to give her a better look and whispered in her ear, "Whatever I do next, play along. You help me and I'll get you out of here if I can. Deal?"

She fiddled with my hair and whispered back. "Why would you do that?"

Eve and I weren't best buds, but I wouldn't wish eternity chained to Lilith's throne on anyone. Not even my enemy. I know what you're thinking, that I was demonstrating good moral character, and maybe I was, but at that moment, I really just wanted to stick it to Lilith in any way possible. Stealing her pet would definitely piss her off, and rescuing Eve would make Adam happy.

And yeah, I didn't want Adam doing something stupid to save Eve and ending up back down here himself.

I hadn't realized Nikita had shifted into her Hell hound state. I heard a growl behind me and the warmth of dog breath brushed against the back of my neck. Still sitting on the floor, I slowly turned my head and saw I was face to muzzle with her.

She bared her fangs.

I bared mine back.

I was sick of her getting in my way, and even though I didn't have my magic, I gave her a hard mental push. "Back the hell off."

The hound's eyes widened. As if someone grabbed her from behind, she slid backwards, nails scraping the floor. Maybe I'd hijacked some of Lilith's energy or Luc had shared his magic, but whatever was healing my body had also given me a psychic jumpstart. I turned back to Eve, meeting her gaze and smiling at my accomplishment.

She didn't seem impressed. Instead, she reared back as if I'd shocked her. "Your eyes…"

I blinked and touched my eyes with my fingertips. My lashes had some dried blood on them, but otherwise felt normal. "What about them?"

"Nothing," she said, but she looked away super quick, and I knew she was lying.

Whatever the issue was, it had to wait. Lilith was still on a rampage, dust and debris starting to fall from the starless ceiling as she stomped her booted feet and continued to throw a temper tantrum. Like Gabe, I was growing tired of the theatrics.

The only way to get Lilith to cough me back up topside and leave me alone was to make myself so annoying, so threatening to her in my dead state, she'd have no choice but to send me back to Earth. I'd already convinced her I wanted to take over her place in Hell. The next thing was to convince her that I would be a better queen and loved by one and all.

Eve helped me stand and I motioned for her to follow me to Lilith's throne. The chair was one heavy sucker and it took us a couple tries to right it, but once we did, I used my new kinetic energy to levitate it back onto the platform. Magic zoomed through my body, a total rush similar to feeling Mikayla's magic flow through me. This was active magic, though, not passive, and I hadn't used any in so long, I felt high.

Lilith's rant died in midsentence as I strode up the stairs and made a production of sitting in her throne.

Once I had everyone's attention, I crossed my legs and drew in a breath, hoping the blood on my face and whatever was wrong with my eyes didn't detract from the regal air I was trying to project. "Yes, I could definitely get used to this," I said. I threw my arms up in the air and the fires all around us blazed high, flames jumping in response to the magic rolling off me. "Release the slaves! Get rid of these awful snakes! And bring me a shoe designer, pronto!"

I laughed as if this was my own personal Disney World and I was Cinderella, the wicked version. "But wait! There's one thing missing. A queen isn't a queen without…"

Glancing over at Luc, I gave him a wicked smile, and slowly, seductively, rose from the throne, strutting down the steps and stopping in front of him. He watched me with a curious expression, wondering what I was up to, no doubt, and since my back was to Lilith, I winked before taking his right hand in both of mine and dropping to my knees.

I bowed my head over his hand. "My king."

His power rose around me, engulfing me in that all too-familiar way. The last of the pain left my body and the sensation of floating filled me. Squeezing my hand, he raised me back into a standing position. As I looked up into his eyes, heat and lust and love sparked between us.

Literally, sparks flew. His heat and my air in a delicious tug of war.

Everything else fell away. Lilith, Gabriel, Eve and Nikita. Hell itself disappeared. There was only me and Luc and the magic between us.

If he'd asked me for my soul at that moment, I would have handed it to him without hesitation. If he'd asked me to truly take Lilith's place and rule Hell with him, I would have done it.

As it was, he asked neither, but there was an unspoken question in his eyes. How far was I willing to carry this charade?

Pretty far, apparently, because I wrapped my arms around his neck, dragged his lips down to mine and kissed him for all I was worth.

You can see now why I have such a hard time staying true to my oath to remain magic-free. Why I struggle with each step of Witches Anonymous. Why I don't deserve Adam.

My moral character is simply…bad.

The kiss rocked me from head to toe, an explosion of sensation lifting me higher and higher. I parted my lips, hungry for Luc's attention. Starved for it. He was more than happy to oblige and we went into full-on make-out mode in front of everybody. I pressed my body against him and he wrapped his arms around me and drew me even closer, the whole time, our lips tasting, teeth nipping, tongues dancing.

Gabe cleared his throat, breaking through the haze of lust in my head. Behind me, Lilith roared with rage, the echo shaking the entire place like an earthquake. With no time to lose, I broke away from Luc and hauled him toward the throne.

"You and me," I shouted over Lilith's bellow. I had to make sure she was at her breaking point. I shoved Luc into the chair and crawled into his lap. "King and Queen of Hell!"

All noise stopped. You could have heard the bell over the door of my ice cream shop ding back in Eden, it was so quiet.

Lilith, veins black with rage, pointed a finger at Gabriel. "Get her out of here!"

Gabe rolled his eyes to the ceiling. "Finally."

Now that it was quiet, I could hear someone calling my name. A whole chorus of people, in fact. "Amy. Amy. Amy," their chants replaced the heartbeat of Hell.

Every call of my name sent magic flowing through me. Innocent magic. Dark magic. White magic. Earth magic.

When Gabriel strolled over and held out one finger toward my forehead, I wasn't sure I even needed his assistance to get back to Earth.

But there's no sense looking a gift angel in the face. "Don't forget Eve," I told him and he shrugged his shoulders as if he cared less who I wanted to bring along.

Luc smiled at me and I smiled back, and just before Gabe touched his finger to my forehead, Luc lowered his mouth and kissed me goodbye.

CHAPTER NINETEEN

I woke in Keisha's guest bedroom again, this time with a bunch of people watching me. Keisha, Liddy and Em formed a semi-circle around the bed. Near the window, which showed it was still dark outside, stood Mikayla, and surprisingly, Nikita, in Rottweiler form, sat at her feet. In the corner, Gabe leaned against the grandfather clock and looked bored. Directly opposite of him was Cephiel who kept one eye on Gabe and the other on Mikayla.

Best of all, there were two warm, furry cat bodies tucked up against mine, both purring with a familiar intensity and rhythm.

As I glanced around, everyone sucked in their breath. The gasp was so audible, I cringed.

"What?" I demanded. "Did I grow a third eye in the middle of my forehead or something?"

My words sounded as though I'd had a shot of Novocain, probably because my bottom lip had swelled into a mountain. Funny, it hadn't felt that big when I'd kissed Luc in Hell.

Keisha leaned forward and studied my eyes carefully and I pressed back into the pillows, afraid she might see some kind of mental replay of that kiss in them. "They're beautiful. So light blue, they're almost white."

"Like a summer sky," Liddy added.

My eyes, blue? No way. My eyes were brown. Not a warm dark brown like Keisha's, not golden brown like Em's. Mine were a dull, boring shade of flat brown.

"I gotta see this." I tried to get out of bed, disturbing the cats, and crying out when a sharp pain cut through my ribcage.

Keisha restrained me and said, "Whoa. You're not going anywhere."

Apparently, now that I was back topside and alive again, my injuries were back too.

Which sucked royally.

She supplied me with a hand mirror from the nearby dresser as Emilia helped me lie back down. I raised the mirror in front of my face, and low and behold, they were right. My eyes were ice blue. Crystalline, with darker blue lines running through them. "Holy Hell."

I looked at Cephiel, then at Gabe. "How did this happen?"

99

Cephiel looked at me like I was a true oddity of nature. "You saw a god, Amy. Saw and touched her and lived."

Shaking my head, I looked in the mirror again. "So what? Eve saw her. She and Nikita touched her. Their eyes didn't turn colors."

"Nikita is a demon," Gabe said, arms crossed over his chest as if annoyed he was here. "Eve has special abilities."

"She's a witch."

He shrugged. "Witch or not, she never tried to best a god."

But I had. I bested her quite well in fact.

Smiling, I brushed my bangs back to see the gash on my forehead had three stitches in it. Around the bright red line, intersecting with the stitched wound, were several squiggly lines forming a sigil of some kind. I touched it lightly with my fingertips and flinched. The stitches were warm, hot almost, and the sigil glowed red for a moment.

"I stitched your forehead," Keisha said, "and wrapped your ribs. Two of them have hairline cracks but they're not broken. Definitely bruised, though. I also bandaged your thigh. Anything else I need to look at?"

Doctor Keisha. She was a handy one to have around. "No, but I could use a mega dose of aspirin and some of that lemon blueberry tea."

"You got it." She looked relieved that I was going to be okay and hustled out of the room.

I caught Cephiel's eyes and pointed at my forehead. "What is this?"

"A safety precaution. Lilith cannot touch you now."

I doubted she wanted to after my stellar acting performance. I probably should be nominated for an Oscar.

"Too bad it's not in the shape of a lightning bolt," Liddy said. "You could be just like Harry Potter."

Yeah, too bad. "Where's Adam? Where's Eve? Did she make it back?"

Em nodded, exchanging a half-worried, half-annoyed look with Liddy. "We haven't seen Adam, but Eve said to tell you thanks. She didn't think you had it in you...you know...to be that nice."

My heart fell over Adam's absence, but Cephiel winked at me and I shoved my disappointment aside. I'd made sure Eve got back, for her and for Adam's sakes. My moral fiber was stronger than I'd thought.

Emilia leaned down to hug me. It was an awkward hug, both because I couldn't sit up, and because neither of us was the demonstrative type. Before she got away, though, I caught hold of her hand and gave it a squeeze. "I love you, Em. I'm sorry about the Barbie playhouse."

Her brows rose, eyes widening as she remembered that day. Years fell away from her face, until she was nine and I was seven again, and then she squeezed my hand back. "Don't ever do that again. Die, I mean. You scared the living daylights out of me. Out of all of us."

I raised my wrist, bandaged I assumed because in this world, it had been ripped open by Nikita, and pointed a finger at the dog. "Blame her. She's the one who killed me and took me to Hell. What's she doing here, anyway?"

For a second, I thought I'd suffered brain damage, because Nikita opened her mouth and said, "Thanks to you, Lilith fired me."

I glanced at Emilia. "Did the dog just talk?"

Em nodded.

"She also threw me out of Hell." Nikita gave me a hostile once over and licked her lips like I was her next meal. "Who ever heard of a Hell hound being barred from Hell?"

This struck me as inordinately funny. Blame it on the stress or the pain burning in my ribs, which only increased as I laughed, or the fact I'd been raised from the dead. A talking dog, a Hell hound kicked out of a hell. My blue eyes. My fat lip. It was all extremely funny.

"I don't know what to do with...her," Mikayla said. Night was fading and purplish shadows covered the window behind her. She wasn't wearing pigtails that morning but her magic was bound up as if she'd braided it, it was so constricted with fear. "My neighbor isn't coming back and she's...well...a Hell hound."

I returned Nikita's hostile stare. "There's always the animal shelter."

Nikita growled and Cain and Abel both hissed at her. Liddy shook her head, lightning bolts zigging and zagging around it. "You can't take a magical dog to the animal shelter. What if a nonmagical family adopts her?"

I sighed. "Well, she can't stay with me."

"And I have too many cats, or I'd take her." Liddy's face drooped with sadness.

We all looked at Em, who raised her hands in defense. "My place doesn't allow pets."

"What about you?" I said to Cephiel. "Immaculate Conception could use a mascot, couldn't it?"

Cephiel eyed Nikita. "While I have been reinstated as Father Leonard, I don't think bringing a talking dog to live at the church will help my efforts to win over the diocese."

"Maybe your girlfriend can take her."

Cephiel had the grace to blush. "Marcia is not my girlfriend, but I will ask her."

Keisha returned, two aspirin and a mug of steaming tea in hand. As she handed them to me, I noticed Gabriel raise a hand toward the back of Mikayla's head. "Hey," I shouted. "What do you think you're doing?"

Gabe froze at the same time Keisha snapped around to glare at him. "We talked about this. You said you'd leave her alone."

Mikayla, having also whirled around to see Gabe's hand stretched in her direction, gave a small screech and backed toward Cephiel. Ceph stepped forward and put a protective arm out in front of her. I was momentarily proud of him. He was learning.

Angelzilla lowered his hand with an exaggerated sigh. "You don't understand."

Pushing past the pain in my ribs, I sat up. "You keep saying that, but you're wrong. If anyone here can sympathize with you wanting to stay on Earth, it's me. But I won't let you possess an innocent witch to do so."

"Possess her?" Keisha staggered. Even a voodoo priestess isn't big on possession. "I thought you just wanted to strip her of her magic. Why in the world would you want to possess her?"

Gabriel gave her a petulant look. "I cannot remain on Earth any longer without a human body to possess." He glanced at the glowing window. "My time is nearly up."

"I thought you had until the full moon," I said.

"The timeline was moved up after I went to Hell to retrieve you."

Oh. Keisha, eyes wide, glanced at me. What could we do, though, outside of sacrificing Mikayla?

My best friend was going to be broken hearted without him, and while he was pain in my ass, he had brought me back from the dead.

I looked at my guardian angel. "Is there any other means to turn him into a human?"

Cephiel pursed his lips in disgust. Why any angel, must less an archangel, would want to be human was obviously beyond him. And yet, I saw something in his face that told me there was something he could do.

"Please, Ceph. I'm asking for your help. I promise to listen to your guidance and make better choices if you'll help Gabe find another way to become human."

One of his brows, flecked with a few gray hairs, lifted and he considered me thoughtfully. "Promise?"

I crossed my heart like I'd done with Natasha, the Pyro, on the roof of the ice cream shop, but that didn't seem like enough, so I raised my hand and tried to make the Boy Scout salute or maybe it was the *Galaxy Quest* "Never give up. Never surrender," one, but either way, it worked. "I promise."

He nodded and said to Gabriel, "I'll talk to someone upstairs and see what I can do. I'll return shortly." With that, he vanished and Mikayla gave another screech.

"Hang around all of us long enough," Liddy told her, "and you'll get used to it."

I could see Mikayla was debating hanging around us at all. Couldn't say I blamed her, but I needed to keep her soul safe from Luc and I was still curious about her mother's death.

Plus, she rocked in the kids' birthday department. "You still interested in working at the shop?"

She hesitated, took a deep breath, and nodded.

"Good. The sooner we're open and running again, the better, and I'm going to be on light duty for awhile, so Keisha's going to need all the help she can get."

I gave Gabe a hard look. "You, too. First thing tomorrow, you report for counter duty, got it?"

He made a face, Angelzilla returning. "I don't do *counter duty.*"

"You do if you're human and living in my shop."

"I probably won't even be here tomorrow."

"Cephiel will come through," I said and motioned at Keisha. "Meantime, Keisha can do a binding spell."

Her face lit up. "Think that might work?"

No, but it would give them hope, and as I well knew, hope is powerful magic. "You're the strongest witch I know, Keisha. If Mikayla and Emilia add their magic to yours, you can probably take over the whole damn world."

"World domination." She smiled and nodded her head. "I like it."

I yawned. The past two days and nights had taken it out of me. Emilia herded everyone toward the door. "We'll be downstairs if you need us."

The sunrise continued to push the dark moon shadows back and bathed the area near the window in a pretty light. Even the grandfather clock looked less icky in the soft morning rays. I'm not, in general, an early riser, but that morning, I wanted to see the sun come up. I wanted to watch it illuminate the trees and wake up the birds and the rest of Eden's citizens.

In other words, it was a good day to be alive.

Maneuvering myself out of bed, I managed to slide a chair over to the floor-to-ceiling window so once I had the curtains pulled back, I could sit and see the entire neighborhood. Birds darted here and there. Squirrels, bushy tails wagging, chased each other in the trees. Keisha's condo sat on a hill and if I shifted to the right, I could almost make out my building three blocks away. If the second floor had still been standing, I could have seen it with ease.

Eden was a pretty town with its tree-lined streets and backyard gardens. Looking at the nearby houses, lights flicking on in their windows as people started their days, I decided it wasn't a bad place to be a washed-up witch. I'd taken it for granted before. After dying and going to Hell, I had new perspective and a newfound love for normal and ordinary.

Luc's power rose around me, tingling my nerve endings and waking my magic, safe and sound again next to my heart, before he shimmered into being in front of me. Without a word, he took my hand, kneeled at my feet and bowed his head.

Heart and magic hammered side by side in my chest. What was he doing here? Why was he on his knees, mimicking my acting job in Hell? Surely he didn't think...

His magic, as delicious as Mikayla's, rippled over my skin and filled me with desire and longing. He raised his head, gave me a wicked grin and winked. "My queen."

I'd like to tell you I jerked my hand away and told him to knock it off. I'd like to tell you I thought of Adam, who'd gone to Hell for me. I'd like to tell you I was completely unfazed by the Devil kneeling at my feet and calling me his queen.

I'd be lying.

His lips beckoned to me. His magic caressed mine. Forget the sigil on my forehead, Luc made me feel safe. No harm would befall me as long as he watched over me.

It wasn't the first time I'd had a man at my feet calling me queen. Samson of Samson and Delilah fame, had done a similar thing at Christmas time.

But I hadn't known Samson, had never had the most intense relationship of my entire life with life with him. So for a brief instant, I wondered what it would be like to be Queen of Hell to Luc's King. Sure, Hell wasn't that appealing, but to rule next to Luc, spend eternity with him fascinated me. The allure was undeniable.

My love for Luc was undeniable.

I came *this close* to leaning forward and kissing him. I wanted to. I wanted to kiss him and seal the deal. Kiss him, and with that kiss, say yes to it all. To him. To Hell. To eternity.

But there was still Lilith.

And Adam.

Downstairs I heard the clatter of a skillet, plates and friendly banter as my friends and sister went about making breakfast. Outside the window, birds sang and cars motored by as people went to work.

I shuddered, a wet hotness creeping along the rims of my eyelashes. Forget Hell and Lilith. In the end, my love for Lucifer and my anguish over that love would burn me up inside.

"I was just pretending, you know. In Hell. That was just…"

A faint disappointment flitted behind his eyes, but the smile stayed in place. He knew I was lying. "An act. Yes, I know."

He didn't believe it though. I didn't believe it either. It was important to stick with the premise, though, because I didn't really want to die and go to Hell, even as queen, any time soon. I wanted to be with Luc, but I wanted to be alive, on Earth, with him. "I didn't much care for Hell. It sucked. No offense."

He rose to his feet, a second chair materializing next to mine, and he sat in it, never letting go of my hand. "Why do you think I spend all my time here? On Earth?" He looked out the window, slanting his eyes away from me. "With you?"

"Sometimes, I wish you were just a normal guy. No magic. No angelic history."

"Could we be together then?"

Yes, my heart said.

No, my brain insisted.

"Maybe."

One of his dark brows rose and he glanced at me. "Perhaps I can do that. Be normal."

Yeah, right. And Gabriel could give up ice cream. "You would stop using magic, give up ruling Hell, to stay on Earth with me and be normal."

He nodded. "I would."

Stunned, all I could do was stare at him. "I would never ask you to do that for me."

"You don't need to ask."

Everything inside me was doing a Snoopy happy dance, but this was dangerous territory. Extremely dangerous. Time to change the subject. "Please tell me Lilith was better looking in the beginning."

"She was a…" His gaze went back to the window. "A goddess."

His tone denoted reverence and awe. I remembered how she'd glowed thinking about Adam. Jealousy reared its head. "Yeah, well, she needs a spa weekend in the worst way."

A slow, deep chuckle resonated in his chest, and as it filled the room, I found myself laughing along. We sat like that, staring at Eden as it began another day, my hand in his, and a sweet comfortableness encircling us. As if we'd been together already for a lifetime. As if we were meant to be together for eternity.

It was good, it was nice, and a part of me wished with all my heart it could stay that way.

Luc glanced at my face, concern crossing his features as he took in my lip. "Do you want me to heal you?"

Boy, did I. "My ribs are killing me. Could you at least numb them for awhile?"

"I would have to use magic."

Crap. So much for normal. "One last time?"

He gave me that wicked smile, then leaned forward to touch my ribcage. Suddenly, my forehead burned and his body flew up in the air, like an invisible hand had lifted him. He slammed into the wall and then did a slow slid to the ground.

He looked at me and I looked at him, both of us speechless.

"What the hell just happened?" he finally said.

I got out of the chair, ribs protesting, and crawled over to him. "I don't know. Are you all right?"

"Your forehead glowed right before I ended up over here."

I raised my hand and brushed my bangs out of the way so I could touch my stitches. The sigil was warm under my fingers. "Cephiel put some kind of mark on me. He said it was for protection."

Luc sat forward and examined it. "The mark of Cain."

An involuntary shiver rolled down my spine. "What does that mean?"

Crossing his legs, Luc rubbed a hand over his eyes. "It means proponents of dark magic cannot touch you without being destroyed. What it just issued to me was a warning. If I try to heal you, because my magic is dark, it will obliterate me."

"No."

"Yes."

"You just held my hand and it didn't do anything. Your magic, I felt it rising around me right before you materialized."

"My magic was contained. I wasn't using it on you or trying to harm you in anyway."

Thoughts raced through my head. "How do I get it off? Cephiel can undo it, right?"

"Few people are ever granted God's holy protection, Amy. Cephiel has gone out on a limb to make you one of them. Asking to have it revoked is unwise."

He was so serious, so sad, sitting there staring at me. "Unwise or not, I want it gone."

"Why?" he challenged. "You're safe from me this way. Safe from Lilith."

I don't want to be safe from you. "Can I touch you without it going off?"

One brow arched in question. "As long as I contain my magic."

I held one hand out, fingers splayed. My heart was pushing ninety in my chest. This was a dangerous test, but I had to know if it was possible. "Touch me."

Luc obediently raised his hand, mirroring mine. Slowly we inched them toward each other.

When our flesh made contact, I let go of the breath I was holding and threaded my fingers through his. His eyes darkened, tantalizing and sexy.

"No magic," I warned.

One side of his mouth went up. "Tease."

"Now, for the real test." I leaned my upper body toward him. "Kiss me."

He drew back out of surprise, but only for a second. "What test exactly are we taking?"

"The one to see if you can be normal."

"Ah."

I smiled. He smiled back. Then we edged our lips toward each other at the same slow speed we had our hands. The moment they touched, electricity raced down my back, over my skin. Lightness filled my chest. Heady desire warmed my lower body. I forgot the pain in my ribs, my fat lip.

But there was no magic, no powers. The sigil didn't go off.

Luc and I, possibly for the first time ever, were just too normal human beings who were in love.

I parted my lips and laughed, carefree and happy, into his mouth. He laughed, too, never taking his lips from mine.

Carefully, I crawled into his lap and continued kissing him as if there was no tomorrow.

Welcome to Temptation!
Read all the Witches Anonymous books:

Witches Anonymous, Step 1, A Tickle My Fantasy story

Can a bad witch go good in thirteen steps? Not if Lucifer has his way with her!

Amy Atwood is a witch. Not the harm-none kind…the Satan-worshipping, devil-made-me-do-it kind. But after catching Lucifer in a particularly wicked hex act with her goodie-two-shoes Wiccan sister, Amy does what every self-respecting witch would do. She pops a Dove chocolate in her mouth, ends her affair with the devil, and swears an oath never to use magic again.

She wants to be normal. Human. Even if it means no more fun—and she's looking for a nice, normal guy to complement her new lifestyle. And ice-cream-loving firefighter Adam Foster looks like perfect hero material.

Lucifer, however, isn't about to be nice about letting her go. Stalked by Satan, manipulated by the angel Gabriel—and surprised by Adam's true identity—Amy finds herself up to her black hat in trouble of Biblical proportions…

Jingle Hells, Witches Anonymous, Step 2

Christmas is going to be hell this year.

Word's gotten around Heaven (and Hell) that Amy tricked the angel Gabriel and helped Adam with his second trial with temptation. Now Samson shows up on her doorstep looking for true love, and Delilah's not far behind, insisting she wasn't the one who cut off his hair.

In order to get both of them out of her ice cream shop and back into each others' arms, Amy must become a relationship expert and a detective while completing Step Two of Witches Anonymous. But will believing in a higher power help Amy in her quest, or make matters worse?

Wicked Souls, Witches Anonymous, Step 3

Wicked is as wicked does.

As reformed witch Amy Atwood wrestles with completing the third step of Witches Anonymous—turning her will over to a higher power—she's counting the days to her six-month magic-free anniversary. However, when Gabriel steals half her soul, claiming she's cast a spell on him to keep him from returning to Heaven, the odds of her sticking to her magic-free oath shrink. He demands she break the spell keeping him Earth-bound...or he'll kill her and damn her soul for eternity.

But Amy's not about to go down without a fight. Having once been the Devil's right-hand witch, her soul's already bound for Hell, and while Gabriel now owns half, the other half belongs to Lucifer...and Amy knows exactly how to use Luc to stop Gabe.

While Amy will do anything—outside of using magic—to reunite the halves of her soul, the powers of good and evil also control her free will. As she works to uncover the real witch behind the spell holding Gabriel prisoner, she finds herself back in Lucifer's arms...and her Witches Anonymous goal spinning further and further out of reach.

Misty Evans is also the author of the Super Agent Series

Operation Sheba, Super Agent Series, Book 1

Hotshot spies never die. They just slip undercover.

Julia Torrison—codename Sheba—is keeping secrets. Seventeen months ago she was a CIA superagent, tracking down dangerous terrorists with her partner and lover, Conrad Flynn. A mission was blown, literally, when a bomb Julia built exploded early and Conrad died.

Yanked back to Langley and given a new identity, she is now the Counterterrorism Center's top analyst, spending her days at CIA headquarters and her nights in the bed of her boss. Her former life as a secret agent has been sealed off. Like her heart.

Conrad Flynn—codename Solomon—has his own secrets. For starters, he's not dead. Going under the deepest cover possible, he faked his death to save Julia's life. Now he must tear her life apart and ask her to help him hunt down a traitor: her new love.

Is Con a rogue agent or just a jealous ex-lover? To find out, Julia will have to enter a web of seduction and betrayal to play the spy game of her life using nothing more than her iPod—and her intuition.

I'd Rather Be In Paris, Super Agent Series, Book 2

He makes the rules. She breaks them. This battle of wills just crossed the line...to deadly.

Elite CIA operative Zara Morgan has a reputation as a loose cannon with a penchant for breaking the rules. Now she's got a chance to prove she can be a competent field officer, but the test doesn't end there. She's been paired with sexy covert ops team leader Lawson Vaughn, a man who lives and breathes protocol.

Methodical is Lawson's middle name. He specializes in high-risk search and rescue, not missions that involve tracking down terrorists. Especially while trying to keep the lid on a partner who has a problem with authority and skates by on wits and bravado

110

Even before they get on the plane for Paris they're under each other's skin…and fighting a scorching sexual attraction. Drawn into an unauthorized game of vengeance, Lawson is forced to dance a tightrope in order to protect his partner from their quarry—a terrorist who's about to unleash a biological nightmare on the Muslim world. And Zara is the first target.

With her life, and that of millions of innocent people, on the line, Lawson must become the one thing he despises. A renegade.

Proof of Life, Super Agent Series, Book 3

Blood ties run deepest—and deadliest.

No matter how many times he patches the holes in the wall, CIA Deputy Director Michael Stone can't forget the night a terrorist took him hostage in his own home. Or the mistakes that transformed him into an overwhelming force to keep his country safe. And now that his niece, the daughter of the Republican candidate for President, has been kidnapped just days from the election, Michael vows to do whatever it takes to get her back.

Dr. Brigit Kent, a consultant for the Department of Homeland Security, knows this particular kidnapper well. Exposing him, however, will reveal her sister's secret ties to a terrorist group. The only way to keep her sister safe is to blackmail the sexy, rock-solid deputy director. A move that puts her directly in his line of fire.

Brigit is undeniably beautiful, brilliant, cunning. But is she friend or foe? The answer to that question could break Michael's personal code of honor—and his heart.

Launch, Super Agent Series, Book 4 (coming 2012)

There's more by Misty...

The Secret Ingredient, A Culinary Romantic Mystery with Bonus Recipes

Celebrity chef Katelyn Karr returns to her hometown of Secret, Montana in order to stop an investigative reporter from revealing the truth about her alcoholic father, dead mother and the reason she was run out of town by the socialite Juno family when she was only seventeen.

During a live cooking show at the Juno ranch, her father dies in front of millions of viewers, and suspicion falls on the celebrity diva when the autopsy reveals he was poisoned. Nick Juno, the boy Kate left behind, and who is now mayor, is the only person who can prove her innocence.

Did Kate kill her father on national TV? Nick must untangle the lies and past secrets to figure out if Kate has been framed or slipped her father a secret ingredient that finally put an end to their family dispute.

Bonus recipes are included at the end of the book!

Soul Survivor, Lost Worlds Series, Book 1

Haunted by tragedy, FBI profiler Rife St. Cloud is driven to find the person who brutally attacked six women. Unfortunately the only survivor, Keva Moon Water, has no memory of what happened, and the evidence makes her the prime suspect.

Keva cannot die. She has waited a thousand years to be reunited with the man she loves, whose soul sleeps within Rife. Though he refuses to believe her claims of immortality, there's no denying the passion that burns between them. Keva desperately hopes their sexual connection will be enough to awaken Rife's memories of the love affair that started a war and bound their souls together for all eternity.

But when Keva's own memories come trickling back, she realizes that a future with Rife depends upon confronting the mistakes of the distant past...

Entangled, A Paranormal Anthology

Ghosts, vampires, demons, and more! *Entangled* includes ten suspense-filled paranormal short stories from authors Cynthia Eden, Jennifer Estep, Edie Ramer, Lori Brighton, Michelle Diener, Misty Evans, Nancy Haddock, Liz Kreger, Dale Mayer, and Michelle Miles, plus a *Seven Deadly Sins* novella by Allison Brennan. Stacia Kane contributed the foreword. Formatting and cover art were also donated to the project by Lori Devoti and Laura Morrigan.

All proceeds go to the Breast Cancer Research Foundation. Stories include:

HALLOWEEN FROST by *USA Today* bestselling author Jennifer Estep (author of the Mythos Academy, Elemental Assassin, and Bigtime series)

THE FAT CAT by Edie Ramer (author of Cattitude, Galaxy Girls)

MEDIUM RARE by Nancy Haddock (author of the Oldest City Vampire trilogy)

SWEET DEMON by Misty Evans (author of the Witches Anonymous series)

SIAN'S SOLUTION by Dale Mayer (author of the Psychic Visions and Blood Ties series)

A BIT OF BITE by Cynthia Eden (author of NEVER CRY WOLF and ANGEL OF DARKNESS)

SINFULLY SWEET by Michelle Miles (author of the Coffee House series)

A NIGHT OF FOREVER by Lori Brighton (author of A Night of Secrets and To Seduce an Earl)

FEEL THE MAGIC by Liz Kreger (author of the Part of Tomorrow series)

BREAKING OUT by Michelle Diener (author of the Tudor-set historical suspense novel In A Treacherous Court)

GHOSTLY JUSTICE, an all-new *Seven Deadly Sins* novella by *New York Times* bestselling author Allison Brennan (author of the Seven Deadly Sins series)

And now for a sneak peek at…

REVENGE IS SWEET

A Kali Sweet Urban Fantasy Story

By Misty Evans

Raj Nudra, Vampire King of the Central United States, was waiting for me.

Seated behind a mammoth black desk, Nudra appraised me with flat reddish-brown eyes. Two of his minions flanked his sides, arms crossed, weapons in plain sight. Low level demons, good for muscle but who couldn't think their way out of a coffin.

Nudra leaned back in his chair, long black hair falling across his shoulders as his feminine lips curved up into a smug smile. "Kalina Dolce, what brings you here? Hoping to score front row seats to the concert?" He pointed to a couple of tickets on his desk and then to a bright orange lanyard with a plastic ID protector. "Or perhaps a backstage pass? Word has it, you were once sweet—no pun intended—on Rad Beaumont. If you're looking to hook up again…" He let the suggestion hang in the air.

No one had called me Kalina Dolce since I'd left Rome in 1910. Kali Sweet was more modern, more American, and it didn't remind me every day of what had happened to my family and friends. Didn't make me catch my breath in fear when someone called me by it, or make my gut cramp with guilt when I saw it written on a random envelope in the mail pile.

I shut down the bloody memory the name called up. Now wasn't the time to revisit the past. In fact, it was never a good time to visit the past. Under the circumstances, however, I recognized Nudra's one-two punch. He'd caught me off guard with his use of my old name and knowledge about my relationship with Rad. He obviously had anticipated my visit and planned accordingly.

Blood-sucking bastard.

Rule one when dealing with vampires, always have a ready escape. Leaving the door open, I removed my Bridge badge from the inside pocket of my cape, regaining my composure as I did so. The weight of the shield reassured me. The way the overhead light bounced off the gold reminded me of the responsibility I held. Nudra was king of a bunch of undead vamps. Big deal. I was a member of the Bridge Council and the best damn vengeance demon on the face of planet Earth.

I shoved my badge in his face. Sniffed the air as if he stunk as I flicked the hood off my head. *Italian flair, check.*

Offense taken, he straightened ever so subtly as I glared down at him. "You've crossed the line with humans again, using them as blood slaves. Trafficking them across state lines and selling them to the highest bidders. That's two strikes this year. One more, and..."

"You'll send me to my coffin for a time out?"

East Indian charm, check.

"One more, and the next time you see me, I'll have pliers in my hand."

His flat eyes sized me up, and then he *tsked*. "Such an inhumane way to remove my fangs."

I fished the written warning out of my back skirt pocket and tossed it on the top of his desk. "They're not for your fangs, buddy boy." *American snarkiness, check.* "They're for your balls."

I grabbed my crotch to emphasize my point before backing toward the door. Rule number two, never, *ever* turn your back on a vamp, especially when threatening his vamphood. "I take your balls, you lose your sex drive, and with it your bloodlust will decrease by ninety-nine percent. You'll stop preying on human girls and boys, and a king with no sac is nothing but a figurehead, so you can wave bye-bye to all this power you've amassed. The Council will divide up your kingdom among the other American vampire rulers and your fortune will be doled out to the blood slaves as restitution."

While his DNA gave his skin a warm tone, the vampire disease paled it. The result was a taupey gray, making it impossible to discern whether or not my words were sinking in.

Nudra leaned forward in his chair. "How surprising the Council sends you, its heart and soul, to do its dirty work." Instantly, I felt his power rising around both of us. Sexual power, blood lust, desire all mixed together. "I could use someone like you in my organization, Kalina. Someone with your strength, your influence. That zest for humans you have fits perfectly with mine. The compensation, of course, would be exemplary. You would have everything you ever wanted."

There was only one thing I wanted, and no one, not even God Himself, could give that to me. Once a demon, always a demon.

I stopped in the doorway. "My name is Kali Sweet." Holding up two fingers, I made snipping motions. "Don't forget it or I'll tattoo it into your skin when I cut off your balls."

My nerves jangled as loud as the music in the walls as I moved quickly into the hallway and continued to back toward the stairs. Threatening a vampire king was stupid, but running a human blood slave business was unforgivable, and if it had been me making the call, I would have staked him on the spot. The Council, however, existed for this very reason. Vigilante justice created more problems than it solved.

115

No surprise, Nudra's minions darted out of the office after me a few seconds later, weapons drawn. *Vampire king bluster, check.* Guns won't kill me, but bullets will slow me down. And they hurt like hell.

Adrenaline pumping, I hit the bar of the stairway's door hard with my backside to push it open. I didn't want to engage the minions, but I reached for my trusty whip, curled around my left arm like a bracelet anyway.

I'd just turned to run down the stairs when I smacked into a solid wall.

Where did that come from, my brain screamed as the impact sent me backwards on my butt, back hitting the cold concrete wall and knocking the wind out of me. A guitar landed at my feet, making a funny twanging noise as if someone had run unskilled fingers over the strings.

A vaguely familiar, surprised sounding voice said, "Kali?" and I looked up to see my daily nightmare standing there in the flesh.

Radison Beaumont, in too-worn jeans and a too-tight black T-shirt, gave me a slow once-over with his beautiful gold-colored eyes before his lips quirked to one side in a smile that sent my already hammering heart into overdrive. Beating like a battering ram inside my chest, it rang in my ears and drowned out the bass drum echoing in the stairwell.

My skirt had flipped up to reveal an expanse of skin between the top of my boots and my underwear and Rad's gaze lingered between my legs a second too long before lifting to meet mine. Dozens of warnings went off in my head, but damn if I could find my voice or my extensive repertoire of Italian curse words. I couldn't even find my breath. He looked a little older than the last time I'd seen him, but still perfect to me in every way. Thick black hair, a little too long and mussed, those gorgeous eyes, flawless skin and teeth. Not to mention faultless proportions. Like they'd done every other time I was in the near vicinity of him, my body, mind and heart staged a coup. Traitors.

While it seemed like an eternity before he spoke, it was in reality only another beat of my heart. He held out one long, perfect hand and in his eyes I saw it was more than just an offer to help me to my feet. It was an olive branch. A peace treaty. "I can't believe you're here. Did you come to see m—" He caught himself, thought better of it. "Did you come for the concert?"

It would have been easy, so easy, to slip my hand into his. To forget the past under the spell of those mesmerizing eyes and allow him to help me up. Instead, I pushed myself off the ground, keeping my back against the wall and shoved my skirt back into place.

Before I could answer, Nudra's minions barreled through the door and nearly knocked Rad and me both down the stairs. As the first one reached for me, Rad snapped his fingers and the guitar on the ground jerked upward, tripping the demon and sending him flying face first onto the top stair. Being half-chaos demon, causing trouble was as easy as breathing to Rad.

116

He turned on the second bodyguard and the demon held up his hands and stepped back. Smart. He must have known Rad could bring the entire building down on him if he wanted to. The demon disappeared through the door, a soft clicking sound resonating in the now silent stairwell as the latch snapped into place. My breathing sounded too loud in my ears. The demon at my feet moaned, but didn't move.

As if nothing had happened, Rad turned to me, a smile tugging the skin over the fine bones of his cheeks. Two dimples sprang to life. "Your hair. It's...different."

"Seriously?" I righted my cape, which had twisted to the left when I fell. I kicked the demon on the stairs out of the way. "That's the best you've got after standing me up at the altar three-hundred years ago? My hair is different?"

"It was two-hundred eighty-five years and three days ago." His golden eyes darkened and he grabbed me around the waist, jerking me up against his rock-hard body. His gaze dropped to my lips and I was suddenly seventeen again. "And this is the best way I can think of to say I'm sorry."

Before I understood what he was about to do, *il pistolino* lowered his half-demon, half-human lips to mine and kissed me.

117

ABOUT THE AUTHOR

Misty Evans is the author of four series: the Super Agent romantic suspense series, the light paranormal Witches Anonymous series, the dark paranormal Lost Worlds series, and the Kali Sweet urban fantasy series. The books in her Super Agent series have won a CataNetwork Reviewers' Choice Award in 2008, CAPA nominations in 2009, the New England Reader's Choice Bean Pot Award for Best Romantic Suspense in 2010 and the ACRA Heart of Excellence Reader's Choice Award for Best Romantic Suspense in 2011.

Misty is currently at work on the next books in all her series. She likes her coffee black, her conspiracy stories juicy, and her wicked characters dressed in couture. When not reading or writing, she enjoys hanging out with her husband of over twenty years and their twin sons.

For more about Misty, her books,
free reads and contests, join her online at...

http://www.readmistyevans.com

Tweet with her: @readmistyevans
Chat with her on Facebook at Misty Evans Author

CPSIA information can be obtained at www.ICGtesting.com
Printed in the USA
LVOW111141130512

281506LV00001B/170/P